RUGBY SPIRIT

GERARD SIGGINS

THE O'BRIEN PRESS
DUBLIN

First published 2012 by
The O'Brien Press Ltd,
12 Terenure Road East, Rathgar,
Dublin 6, Ireland.
Tel: +353 1 4923333; Fax: +353 1 4922777
E-mail: books@obrien.ie.
Website: www.obrien.ie
Reprinted 2014.

ISBN: 978-1-84717-333-1
Text © copyright Gerard Siggins 2012
Copyright for typesetting, layout, editing, design
© The O'Brien Press Ltd

2 3 4 5 6 7 8
14 15 16 17

Printed and bound by CPI Group (UK) Ltd, Croydon, CR0 4YY
The paper used in this book is produced using
pulp from managed forests.

The O'Brien Press receives assis

RUGBY SPIRIT

'entertaining from cover to cover'
Irish Independent

'Superbly written … well worth a read'
Irish Mail on Sunday

'brimming with action and mystery'
Children's Books Ireland

'a brilliant read'
Sunday World

'brilliant story for rugby-mad youngsters … its
simple approach ensures it can be enjoyed just as
much by those new to the game'
Sunday Independent

GERARD SIGGINS was born in Dublin and has lived almost all his life in the shadow of Lansdowne Road; he's been attending rugby matches there since he was small enough for his dad to lift him over the turnstiles. He is a sports journalist and worked for the *Sunday Tribune* for many years. His sequel to *Rugby Spirit, Rugby Warrior,* is also published by The O'Brien Press.

DEDICATION

Friends are everything – I dedicate this to Martin McAllister for being the best you could have.

ACKNOWLEDGEMENTS

Thanks to Dad, Mam, Kieran Hickey and Martin Coonan for encouraging me to write; thanks to Harry, Deryck, Sharon and Andrew for their help and advice; thanks to Jack, Lucy and Billy for being my front row; and thanks to Martha – for everything.

CHAPTER 1

The pain in Eoin Madden's stomach grew worse as his dad drove up the driveway. Maybe it was the tall trees leaning in on the narrow avenue; maybe it was the grey stone building that rose at the end of the road, but Eoin's first impression of his new school was ruined by that horrible knot in his belly.

'There's the rugby pitch,' said his dad, 'Grandad was a bit of a star there in his day.'

'But you weren't much good at sport, Dad, were you?' joked Eoin.

'No, but I got my head into the books and don't you forget that's the main reason you're in school,' his Dad shot back, with a wide grin on his face.

Mr Madden parked the car on the end of a line of big cars that all had registration dates from the previous year or two. Eoin felt mildly embarrassed that his dad hadn't changed his car in almost a decade, but he understood that there wasn't much money in a small farm in County Tipperary.

They had left Ormondstown at 6am, stopping only for a barely-nibbled snack on the way. The pair chatted on the journey up to Dublin, going over the weekend's sports results and recalling the best days of the long, warm summer.

But that was all a far-off memory for Eoin when he stepped out of the car and looked up at the front of the school and the enormous crest in a language he could only guess was Latin.

'*Victoria Concordia Crescit,*' boomed a loud voice from somewhere just behind Eoin. 'Victory comes from harmony!'

Eoin turned to see a small, bald man walking towards him with his arm outstretched.

'Good morning, Mr Madden. And you, my lad, must be Master Madden.'

Eoin looked the man up and down. They didn't shake hands at his old school. He realised his mouth was wide open.

'I'm Mr McCaffrey, and I don't bite,' smiled the teacher, as Eoin eventually stuck out his right hand. 'I'm the headmaster of Castlerock College. You're very welcome to the school. I taught your father, and I hope you will be as good a pupil as he was …'

His dad's ears turned bright pink.

'… and as good a rugby player as your grandfather. I was a first-year pupil the year he almost single-handedly won the Senior Cup for the school. It was one of the most amazing performances ever seen at Lansdowne Road. We were all sure he'd play for Ireland one day, but of course …' he trailed away.

'How is your father?' he asked Mr Madden.

'He's not so good,' Eoin's dad replied, 'his health has been poor, he doesn't get out much at all nowadays.'

'I'm sorry to hear that,' said Mr McCaffrey, 'please give him my best. Now Master Madden, we'll have to get you settled. Do come inside.'

Eoin walked through the dark wooden doors, glancing up at the motto once more, 'Victory comes from harmony,' he said to himself, 'hope I get a bit of harmony anyway.'

Inside, Mr McCaffrey scurried across the highly-polished floor to his office.

'This is my office, I presume you won't be visiting me here too often,' he joked.

Eoin forced his mouth into a smile.

'Now, let's see what we have in store for you,' he said as he opened a thin brown cardboard file. 'You're now twelve years old, which means we won't be starting you in the senior school until next year. You will be a member of the Sixth Form and I trust a starring member of the Under 13 school team. What position do you play exactly?'

'Eh, I play centrefield,' replied Eoin.

'*Centrefield* ... what's centrefield?' puzzled Mr McCaffrey.

'In gaelic...'

'Ah, I understand, you play *GAA football*,' said the headmaster, curling up his nose as if a herd of cattle had just passed his window. 'Well, we don't play that sport. It's all rugby here. But you're a strapping lad, I'm sure you'll fit in well. We have three teams in each year so you can learn the ropes.'

'Yes, sir,' said Eoin. 'I'm looking forward to that.'

But, really, he wasn't looking forward to it at all. Rugby was a mystery to him. Sure, he knew all about Brian O'Driscoll and Paul O'Connell, and had cheered to the rafters when Ireland won the Triple Crown the year before. But he hadn't a clue about these positions with their strange names like 'hooker' and 'flanker', and was never sure what each of them was supposed to be doing at any given time.

He had heard that his grandad had been a bit of a star, but he never wanted to talk about it whenever Eoin asked. Grandad was funny like that: he was a very kind, generous and friendly man, but was reluctant to talk about himself and always changed the subject when rugby came up.

Then, one day earlier in the year, after they watched Munster win a thrilling Heineken Cup game on TV, he asked Eoin if he had any interest in playing the game; when he said he did, his grandad said he would see what he could do.

The next thing Eoin knew, his father and mother were telling him that he'd been accepted for a place in Castlerock College up in Dublin, and that he would be starting in September.

The summer went with a blur, and after a few hard goodbyes to his pals, here he was in this strange – slightly scary – school a hundred miles from home.

'I'll be fine, Dad,' said Eoin, when they got outside. The boy drew himself up to his full height as he looked his father in the eye. 'I'll work hard, I promise,' he said, breaking into a grin after half a second.

'OK, well, don't forget to ring your mother when you get a chance. Have you enough money?'

'I do, Dad, please stop worrying.'

His father looked down at the ground. 'Well, look after yourself and I'll see you next weekend.'

As his dad drove away, Eoin bit his lip, but quickly shook himself and turned to look once again at the grey facade.

'Off you go, Master Madden,' he said to himself, 'this is what you're going to have to call home for the next seven years.'

He found his dormitory without difficulty, as it was the first room inside the door on the top storey of the main building. Inside he found six beds with lumpy pillows and ugly green duvets. There were suitcases and kitbags on each bed except the one in the far corner, which he headed for.

As he walked along the row, he noticed a strange scuffling noise, which he realised was coming from under one of the beds. He stooped and peered into the dark space, where he spied a scruffy, blond head topped with a red woolly cap.

'Come out Mighty, pleeeeease,' cried the figure.

'Eh, who's Mighty?' asked Eoin.

'Oh, gosh, I'm sorry,' said the boy. 'Mighty's my mouse. And he's missing.'

'I gathered that,' said Eoin. 'Where did he go?'

'He jumped down off my locker and scarpered. I think he's underneath your bed.'

'That's all I need,' thought Eoin, as he got down on his hands and knees to help his new room-mate.

Eoin spotted the little brown creature and moved slowly but surely towards him. He looked the mouse in the eye, transfixing him, before he pounced, snapping his hands down like an overturned cup and trapping the pet.

'Wow, that's some trick,' said the boy, 'where did you learn that?'

'Down home,' shrugged Eoin, 'it's what we farm boys do.'

'Thanks, that was really cool,' said the boy, as he retrieved his pet from Eoin's upturned hands.

'No problem. By the way, I'm Eoin Madden. I've just arrived.'

'Oh, sorry, I'm Alan Handy,' said the boy, 'we heard there was a new boy coming. Alvaro used to sleep there, but he had to go home to Portugal when his dad got sick.'

'Sorry to hear that,' said Eoin, 'what was he like?'

'He was OK, but he cried a lot at night – I hope you won't be like that,' he grinned.

'I hope not,' laughed Eoin. 'I suppose I'll miss home,

but I doubt it'll be enough to make me cry.'

He lifted his suitcase and sports bag onto the bed.

'I'm starving. I suppose there's no room service up here?' he joked.

'Eh, no, but I've a Bounty bar if you want to share,' said his room-mate.

The pair sat on their beds munching the chocolate as Eoin took in his surroundings.

'Have you been here long?' he asked.

'Four years now,' said Alan. 'It's not too bad if you get in with a nice bunch. There's a few lads you'll need to avoid, but if you do that you'll enjoy it. Do you play rugby?'

'Not yet,' admitted Eoin. 'I don't mind giving it a go, but I've never even seen a real ball up close before. It seems to be a big thing here, is it?'

'Bigger than anything,' said Alan. 'The teachers are all obsessed with it. The school has been pretty successful over the years, but we haven't won the cups for eight or nine years now. We've had some pretty good players, but always seem to blow it.'

'Yeah, I got the impression Mr McCaffrey was more interested in what position I played than whether I could read and write!'

Alan laughed. 'Well, I suppose with your pedigree he

must have great hopes ...'

Eoin stopped and turned to stare at his room-mate.

'What do you mean – how do you know about my pedigree?'

Alan was embarrassed, 'Sorry, I only realised it a minute ago. The head told us that the grandson of Dixie Madden was coming to join our year so I worked out that must be you.'

'Dixie Madden. You know my grandad too?'

'No, I've never met the man. But it's been hard to avoid Dixie Madden for the last four years. Did you not see the sign?'

Eoin turned and looked as Alan pointed to the entrance to the room. A polished wooden plaque hung on the door bearing the words 'The Dixie Madden Dormitory.'

CHAPTER 2

Eoin stared at his grandfather's name and marvelled at how Dixie was so obviously revered up in Dublin when his rugby days were never mentioned at home in Ormondstown. He smiled as he thought of how kind his grandad was to him and nice it was that he was so respected by these people. But he frowned as he remembered how little he knew about Dixie's rugby career.

'Did you not know about that?' asked Alan.

'No, Grandad never really talks about himself,' replied Eoin.

'Well, you'll hear all about him here; he's one of the names the old teachers always bring up.'

Eoin didn't know what to say, he was a bit embarrassed that this virtual stranger knew more about his grandfather than he did. He changed the subject.

'When do we start playing rugby?'

'After school tomorrow, I expect,' replied Alan, 'We usually train two days a week and have matches on Wednesday afternoons and Saturday mornings. I'm not really that good, so I expect they'll start me on the Cs. I suppose you'll start there too, Dixie or no Dixie!'

Eoin smiled.

'Yeah, to be honest I'm a bit nervous abut it. Like I said, I've never even handled a ball. I watched a few big games on the TV, but I'm totally confused by all the positions. Can you help me out there?'

'No problem,' grinned Alan, grabbing a copybook from his locker.

'OK, you do know it's fifteen-a-side? Well, the team is divided into seven backs and eight forwards. The forwards are called 'the pack' and when they have a scrum the team lines up like this.'

Alan drew a basic plan with numbers and letters:

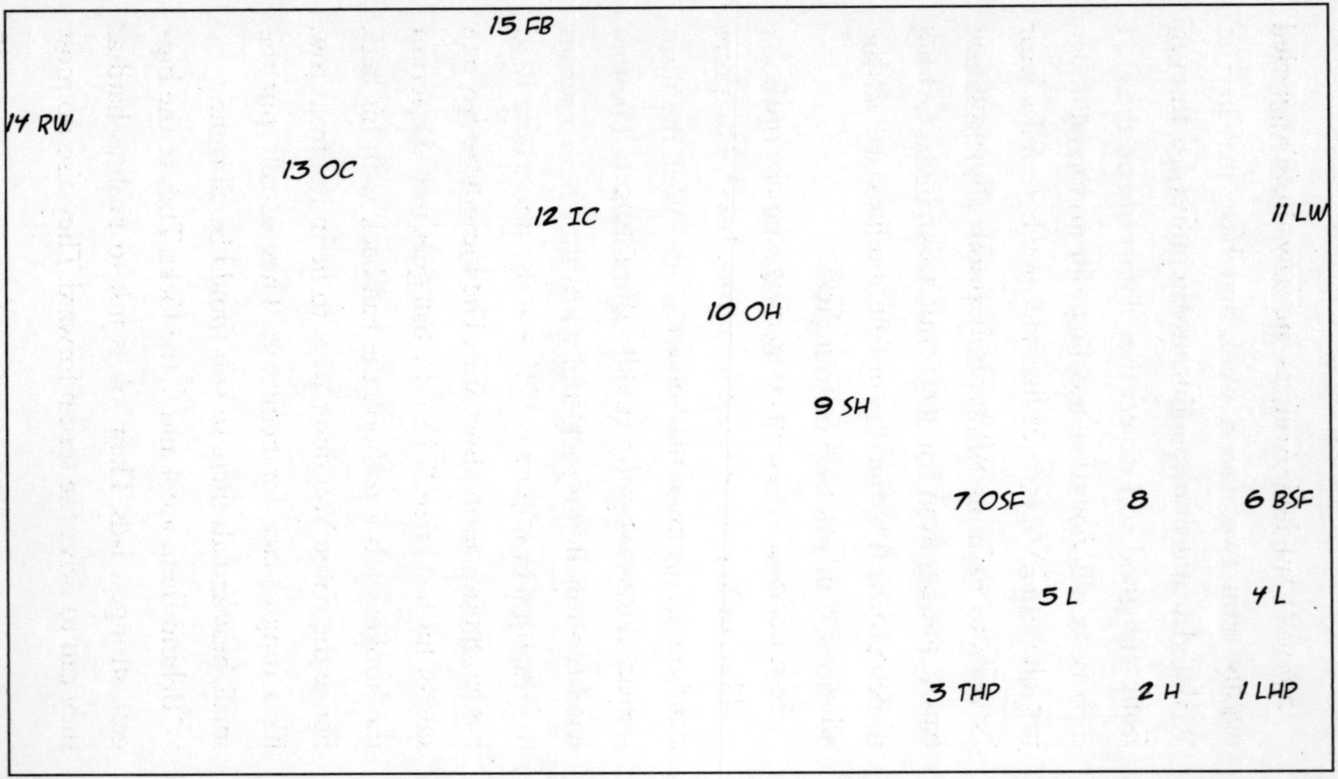

15 FB

14 RW

13 OC

12 IC

10 OH

9 SH

11 LW

6 BSF

8

7 OSF

5 L

4 L

2 H

3 THP

1 LHP

'Simple!' laughed Alan, as he saw Eoin's puzzled expression.

'I'm glad *you* think so. I'm more confused than ever,' Eoin replied.

'It's easy,' said Alan. 'Each of the positions has a number, just like in GAA. It's not like soccer where fellas wear No.23 or No.14 or whatever. If you're a forward you have a number from 1 to 8 on your back, if you're a back it's 9 to 15. And whatever number you have will decide what job you have to do on the field.'

Eoin nodded, the numbers starting to make sense.

'The last line there is the front row, 1-2-3. The props stand on each side of the hooker.'

Alan interlocked the middle three fingers on each hand to show how the front rows met.

'The tight head prop – THP – is the one whose head has an opponent on either side. The loose head has one side of his head free. When the ball goes into the scrum the hooker's job is to hook the ball back with his heel, hence the name. You don't want to be in the front row, it's a rough place for beginners. They usually put the small, heavier lads there so you should be all right.

'Behind them are 4 and 5, the locks. They're the biggest, strongest lads. Their job is just to push as hard as they can to drive the scrum forward. They also do most of the jumping in the line-out.

'The back row has 6-7-8, or actually 6-8-7.'

'Yeah, I was wondering about that,' said Eoin. 'You don't have any letters beside the number eight.'

'Genius,' said Alan. 'The number eight is actually called the Number Eight. For some reason they haven't given him a name. He's another big lad who helps drive the scrum. He'll also be good at handling the ball – Jamie Heaslip does that for Ireland and Leinster. He's my favourite player.'

'Yeah, he's pretty good,' lied Eoin, making a mental note to do some serious homework on the Irish team.

'The other two are the wing-forwards, also called the flankers. They are different roles, there's a blind-side – see, he's the BSF – who lines up nearest the touchline: on the pro teams he'll be big and a strong tackler, the open-side has more chance to go on the attack so he'll be smaller and faster.

'Why have they got two names, wing-forward and flankers?' asked Eoin.

'Haven't a clue,' said Alan. 'We had this coach from New Zealand for a few weeks last year. He kept going on about 'breakaways.' When he introduced us to the 'fly-half' and 'first five-eighths' we hadn't a clue what he was on about. Just call them 'flankers' for the moment, with a bit of luck you won't be asked to play there.

'Our coach will be Bandy Carey, and he'll probably put you in the backs. We'll have a chat about them after practice tomorrow if you like?'

'Yeah, thanks,' said Eoin, 'that'd be great. So, what do boys do for crack around here on a Sunday afternoon?'

'Eh, usually watch rugby on TV,' replied Alan.

'Oh dear, I really hope I get to like this game,' sighed Eoin.

The dormitory door swung open and in streamed four boys.

'Hi, Alan,' they all called out, before catching sight of Eoin.

'Oh, you're new,' said a small boy with curly red hair. 'I'm Rory.'

'I'm Eoin, nice to meet you all. I've taken the last bed there, I hope that's OK?'

With a chorus of 'No problem,' the other three introduced themselves as Kevin, Anton and Fiachra before they began unpacking their bags.

'They all seem grand,' Eoin muttered to Alan.

'Yeah, they're sound,' replied Alan, 'Now let's go off and find some of this "crack" you're looking for.'

Alan led the way downstairs to a large room where boys of all shapes and sizes were to be seen. Some were watching a soccer match on TV, but most were sitting in groups chatting over the summer gone by and the school year ahead.

This is the junior common room, the JCR. Our form is allowed to use it this year – actually this is *my* first time in here, too – and the rest of the guys are from classes up to Junior Cert. The SCR is just for the Leaving Cert guys. They say there's a full bar in there and they all drink beer and smoke cigarettes, but I've never met anyone who's been inside it.'

Eoin looked around the walls at dozens of photographs of school rugby teams. He supposed Dixie Madden would be here somewhere. What year would he have been here? He must ask Mr McCaffrey.

'Hi, Handy!' roared one boy across the room, 'that's some stupid hat you're wearing.'

'Hmmph. Hello, Richie,' replied Alan.

'Who's your new buddy then?' Richie asked.

Rather than conduct a long-distance conversation, Alan walked across to the armchair in the corner where Richie Duffy, wearing a Chelsea shirt, was surrounded by a gang of grinning boys.

'This is Eoin, he's new. He comes from Tipperary.'

'Wow, a real-life bogger,' laughed Richie. 'We don't get too many carrot-crunchers in this school.'

Eoin stared at him, silently.

'Doesn't say much, does he?' sneered Richie.

'I'm choosy,' said Eoin.

'Well, it's good to hear that,' said Richie. 'I suppose we'll be seeing you at rugby tomorrow then. Or are you more of a camogie player?'

Richie's gang chuckled.

'I'll be there,' said Eoin, turning slowly away as Alan quickly headed for the exit.

'That Richie Duffy's a creep,' he explained. 'He's a bit of a mouth and he picks on the younger kids. He's sneaky though, he never gets caught. He's one of the ones you need to avoid.'

'I can't see why I wouldn't,' said Eoin, 'he's not my type.'

'It'll be hard though,' sighed Alan. 'He's the best rugby player in our year and he's sure to be made captain of the 13As.'

Alan showed Eoin around the school and its grounds, giving him lots of useful tips on shortcuts, places to hide and places to steer clear of. They ended the tour in the enormous dining hall, which was just opening for the first dinner of the new term. The pair joined their room-mates for a simple, but not-very-tasty dinner of pork chops. It reminded Eoin of home as he imagined the fine roast dinner his mum would be serving up back in Ormondstown.

The six headed back up to their room, belching and joking as they went.

'Lights-out is nine o'clock for our year,' said Kevin, 'so make sure you're ready for bed or you'll be tripping up in the dark. Don't get caught outside after nine or there'll be war.'

Eoin settled down and chatted with Alan, whose bed was beside his. It had been a full, interesting day, but tomorrow would be even more so. With so much bouncing around his head, it was a wonder Eoin found time to sleep at all.

CHAPTER 3

H is first day as a pupil of Castlerock College passed quickly for Eoin. It was funny having a different teacher for each subject, and they all singled him out for attention as 'the new boy', but they all seemed very nice as they settled into the new school year.

He stuck close by the rest of his room-mates, exchanging no more than the odd 'hi' with the rest of the class.

The last class of the day was History, and Eoin was already starting to yawn before the teacher even walked into the classroom. He wasn't used to these longer schooldays, and he was itching for some fresh air and a bit of a run-around.

'My, my, there's a healthy set of tonsils,' announced the teacher who had suddenly appeared in the doorway.

Eoin went bright red.

'I assure you that you won't be yawning by the end of my highly-stimulating class,' the teacher smiled. 'And you, of course, must be young Madden.'

'Yes, sir,' he confirmed, for the eighth time that day.

Eoin smiled thinly at the man, who was tiny and seemed *very* old indeed.

Richie Duffy raised his head and turned back to stare at Eoin. He looked puzzled.

'I must say, it is a great honour to be teaching a second member of such an illustrious family,' said the teacher.

Richie looked even more bewildered.

'Do you young gentlemen know that I once played scrum-half to the greatest out-half this school has ever seen?,' the teacher asked the room.

'Yes, sir,' the class chorused. 'You tell us this story *every* year.'

'Well, you may not know this yet, but the grandson of the great Richard "Dixie" Madden is sitting among you.'

The class turned as one and stared at Eoin, who felt his red face get hotter and feared it must now look almost purple.

'Wow,' said a couple of boys. 'That's really cool.'

'Tell us about him, Eoin,' said Kevin, sensing a chance to delay having to open the books at the Tudor Plantation.

Eoin wanted the desk to open and swallow him up.

He felt his face turn from red to white.

'OK, gentlemen, settle down,' said the teacher, sensing Eoin's discomfort. 'There'll be plenty of chances to hear all about the Senior Cup Team of 1964. For now, let us turn to page one of your reader and that loveable rogue Henry the Eighth. If you behave yourselves I'll tell you all about the bits they wouldn't put in the sixth-class textbook.'

Eoin greatly enjoyed Mr Finn's colourful History class, a subject he hadn't previously had any interest in at all.

As the class ended, the teacher asked him to stay back for a moment.

'I just wanted to apologise for putting you on the spot like that. I should have known better. I haven't seen Dixie for a few years now, but my guess is that he has never told you of his exploits on the rugby-football field. He was always very reticent about blowing his own trumpet. A very modest man, very private ...' his voice trailed away. 'Now, off to Mr Carey with you. He's a great coach and will bring to the fore any rugby genes you've inherited. Best of luck and, again, my apologies.'

Eoin dumped his books in his desk and, grabbing his kitbag, dashed out to the sports ground where some of his class were already tossing the ball around.

An enormous man with a clipboard was standing outside the changing room, ticking off the names as the boys ran out.

'.... Duffy, Handy, O'Leary, Swarbrigg, Hardiman, Vincent ... That seems to be everyone.'

Eoin dashed past him into the changing room.

'Hello! Who are you and why are you late?' asked the coach.

'I'm Eoin Madden, sir. I'm sorry, but Mr Finn kept me back and—'

'—Well Mr Madden,' interrupted the coach. 'That's not a great start is it? In trouble with the teachers on day one, and now late for rugby practice. If a player is late for my practices he is automatically dropped down to the team below. Of course that doesn't really apply as you're starting on the 13Cs anyway. Just don't be late *ever* again.'

Eoin opened his mouth to reply, but thought better of it.

'Yes, sir,' he replied as he turned into the dressing room to change into his green and white kit.

By the time he ran out onto the field Mr Carey had already divided the boys into three groups of about twenty. He pointed Eoin in the direction of the third group, the largest, which included Alan and Rory and seemed to have more boys wearing glasses than he had ever seen on any sports team.

'Glad to have such rugby pedigree on our humble team,' joked Alan as Eoin joined the 13Cs.

'All right, settle down,' roared Mr Carey. 'And welcome back to you all, and a special welcome to our new 13C star, Mr Madden.'

Eoin glared at Richie Duffy, who he saw sniggering in the first group.

'OK, as it's the first day back we'll have a practice match between the As and Bs after we do our warm-up. I hope you all worked a bit on your handling skills in the summer. I'll take a look at the 13Cs and see if there's any bit of talent here I haven't noticed before.'

After the boys warmed up Mr Carey directed the 13Cs to the second pitch and asked a sixth year to referee the 13A v 13B game.

'Now gentlemen, you have to remember that we're not playing mini-rugby anymore. This is the real thing, or as near the real thing as most of you will ever get. The Cs will be playing one game a week, and I expect all of you to turn out for every training session. This school is going to win a Leinster cup in the next few years, and although it's highly unlikely that any of you lot will be on the team, it's important that you work hard at your game to give the school greater strength in depth.'

'Encouraging, isn't he?' whispered Eoin to Alan.

'All right, let's divide you up into forwards and backs,' said Mr Carey, directing the boys into two groups. Eoin was pointed towards Alan and Rory.

'What does this mean, guys?' he asked.

'You're in the backs with us,' replied Rory. 'It's a lot easier than being up front with forwards with your head wedged between two bums.'

'Right, forwards – off you go to Mr Doyle over there. He'll run you through your paces. The rest of you, come with me.'

CHAPTER 4

Mr Carey gathered the 13C backs together in the lower end of the rugby field.

'Right lads, we're going to line up two sets of backs and practise a few running and passing drills. Nothing fancy, keep it simple.'

He handed out green and orange bibs, quickly allotted the players their positions, and they all scurried off into place.

'Madden, you go full-back.'

Eoin hesitated, wishing Alan hadn't started his rugby lesson with the forwards the night before.

'Where's that, sir?'

'Gosh, you're a bit raw, aren't you,' said Mr Carey. 'You're at the back there, right in the middle. We'll just use half the pitch so stand on the half-way line to start with.'

The teacher tossed the ball to Rory, the scrum-half,

who passed it to the out-half who moved it on to the inside centre. The ball travelled out along the back line to the winger, before it came all the way back again. After two or three turns the ball was passed over to Eoin's team who did the same exercise.

When the ball first came to Eoin he was surprised how easy it was to catch hold of it and pass it on. The awkward shape came comfortably into your arms if you didn't snatch at it. Maybe it wouldn't be too bad after all.

A couple of the boys fumbled their passes or dropped the ball, but Eoin was delighted that he had so far managed to do everything right.

'Right, I want the orange bibs team to do it now, with the green team defending. Just touch tackling now, nothing too rough,' said Mr Carey.

The ball went along the line again, with the players having to pass the ball as soon as one of the green team touched him. Eoin was fast on his feet and was able to stop most attacks in their tracks.

'OK now, let's change it around,' shouted the coach, 'I want to see a bit more commitment from you guys.'

The green team out-half, a nervous-looking boy called Edward Robinson came under pressure from his opposite number and hurled the ball hard and high over his right shoulder. The inside centre had to leap in the air to try to reach the ball, but only succeeded in tapping it even higher, in the direction of the full-back.

Eoin sensed the orange players charging towards him, but with a powerful kick of his heels he leapt high into the air. He was so excited by the action that he just couldn't stop what happened next.

He reached for the ball, far above the outstretched arms of the other boys, and held tight as it came into his hands. He descended to earth, where he looked at the bewildered faces of the boys in orange. With a quick sidestep he dodged around the opposition before he kicked the ball out of his hands towards the goalposts.

The game stopped, with players on both sides staring open-mouthed as the ball floated high over the crossbar.

'Oh no, what was that?' asked Alan, through gritted teeth.

'What are you doing?' asked Mr Carey, with far greater volume. 'This isn't Croke Bloody Park!'

Eoin felt two feet tall, and shrank even further when he heard the guffawing from the touchline, where the 13As and Bs were watching.

'Mooooooooo,' went Richie Duffy, as the rest of his gang followed up with more farmyard noises.

'I'm sorry, sir, I forgot where I was for a moment,' Eoin blurted.

Carey stopped for a moment, staring at Eoin.

'OK, son, just remember this is rugby. We have a bit of work to do with you yet.'

He turned towards the oinking spectators on the touchline.

'All right you lot, the show's over. Get back to work. Extra laps for the last man I see.'

The coach turned back to the Cs.

'You boys can knock off for the day. I'm quite impressed – there's hope for some of you. Madden, come to see me after homework.'

Eoin grimaced again, as his first day at Castlerock just seemed to get worse and worse.

In the changing room he was silent, refusing to respond to Rory's gentle ribbing. Alan hung back afterwards.

'You OK, Eoin? That was a bit mad what you did, but it was pretty impressive too. Cheer up, it will be easier from now on.'

Eoin shrugged, keeping his thoughts to himself as the pair walked back to school.

Homework was easy enough, with just a small amount of written work for the first day back. All through the study period, however, Eoin kept thinking about his leap for the high ball and how dopey he had been.

'Still,' he laughed to himself, 'that was some point. That would have brought the house down if I'd done it for Ormondstown in the county final!'

CHAPTER 5

Eoin stood up and yawned.

'Better get this over with,' he grinned at Alan, who wished him luck.

He scurried down the stairs to the ground floor, where the staff room was situated next to the head-master's office. He knocked once, and the door opened immediately.

'Good evening, Mr Madden,' said the rugby coach, who towered over him. 'Let's take a walk.'

Mr Carey led the way out the main door and out towards the rugby field. He stopped at the nearest touchline.

'We got off on the wrong foot today, so let's leave that behind us. As you know, my name is Brendan Carey, and I'm in charge of coaching rugby for all the sides up to the Junior Cup team. I won't be seeing much more of the 13Cs to be honest, but then again neither will you,

I expect.'

Eoin gulped, 'Well … I enjoyed playing with them, they're a nice bunch of lads.'

'Look, Madden, I'm a firm believer in great rugby players being born, not made. The great players that came through here? I spotted them all on their very first day. Even in your, eh, *moment of madness* today you showed extraordinary ability at two very important aspects of the game, catching and kicking. Once you settle in and learn the game I'll put you up to the Bs. I fully expect you to be on the 13As by Christmas.'

Eoin stared at his shoes. 'Well, sir, as you might have guessed, that was the first time I ever played rugby. I don't know how I could be any good.'

'Listen, Madden,' replied the coach, 'like everyone else here I've heard all the stories about your grandfather. If great rugby players are born, well, you certainly have a head start on anyone else. However, we have a bit of schooling to do with you on the ins and outs of the game.' He took a small, green book from his pocket. 'This is a bit out of date, none of the experimental laws are in it – actually, I think it still says it's four points for a try and that went out about twenty years ago – but it will give you the basics.'

He handed the book to Eoin who looked at the tatty

cover. *Rugby for Young Players: a guide by Andrew Finn.*

'Your History teacher, Mr Finn, wrote it,' explained the coach. 'He was a fine player in his day.'

Eoin thanked Mr Carey and promised he would look after it.

'You can hang onto if you like. These days we get boxes of DVDs, folders and action packs sent out by the IRFU every season. But I think Mr Finn's book is a great primer for a lad new to the game. Right then, off you go, and I'll see you at training on Wednesday.'

The coach turned and walked to his car, which was parked on the kerb. Eoin smiled as he realised it was the same make and model as his dad's. Maybe there were families and people just like him in Dublin after all.

Clutching the little green book, Eoin took the stairs two at a time on his way to the dorm.

Eoin pressed his fingers against his grandfather's name and whispered 'thanks' as he opened the door.

'OK, bud,' said Alan as he entered. 'How did it go?'

'Well…' started Eoin. 'I'm still not sure. I thought I was going to get a lashing, but instead he told me I was a pretty good player. In the end he gave me a book!'

Alan's eyes widened. 'You jammy sucker,' he chuckled. 'Bandy Carey can be very tough on anyone he doesn't like. It looks like your luck is holding.'

'Yeah, but I suppose he did give me some extra study,' Eoin said as he tossed the little green book on the bed. 'How about you fill me in a bit on what the backs do, Alan? It might have been more useful today than that forwards stuff.'

'Yeah, I was thinking that when you were doing your Henry Shefflin stuff ...'

'Henry Shefflin? He's a hurler! Does anyone up here know anything about Gaelic games? It was *football* I was playing down in Ormondstown. And I wasn't a bad footballer, either.'

'Well,' said Alan, 'You better forget all that stuff till next summer. This is rugby town and you're about to become a fully paid-up citizen. I'll draw you the way the backs line up again,' he said, reaching for another copybook.

'So, 15 is the full-back, where you were playing today.

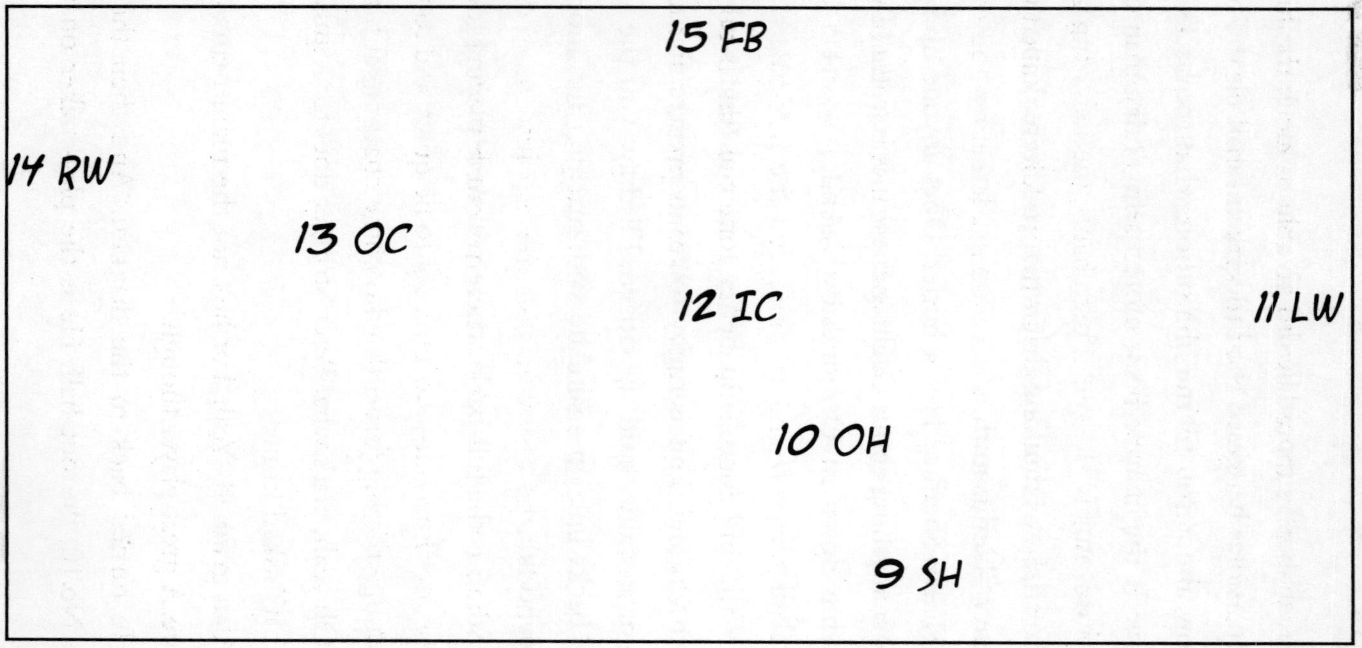

11-LW

9 SH

10 OH

12 IC

15 FB

13 OC

14 RW

Guys who play there have to be able to catch the high balls and have a good boot to kick the ball clear. Then comes the three-quarters line,' he said, drawing a line between the numbers 14, 13, 12 and 11. The outside ones are usually the speed merchants, the left wing and right wing, while the ones in the middle are called the centres – see here they're called inside centre and out-side centre.

'The inside centre is called that because he's just inside when the out-half passes the ball back.

'That pair at 9 and 10 are called the half-backs,' he said, drawing another line. 'They are the link between the backs and the forwards, and teams pretty much run the game from there.

'The No.9 is the scrum-half, usually a small, nippy player. He's the one who puts the ball into the scrum and then collects it when it comes out his side. It's the same after line-outs, too. He's got to be quick and tough to dodge the big forwards who come charging at him.'

'Oh yeah, that's what Peter Stringer does for Munster, isn't it?' asked Eoin.

Alan grinned, 'Yeah, but he's not the main man any-more. A great player though.'

He turned back to the diagram. 'And then there's the No.10, the out-half. He is the play-maker on the team. As long as the scrum-half gets the ball back to him quickly, he can make all the calls on whether he kicks, runs or passes. If you have a good out-half you're well on your way to a winning team. Ireland and Munster had Ronan O'Gara these past few years and look how well they did.'

Eoin nodded, recognising O'Gara's name.

'You saw the way Carey got us to sling the ball along the line today. That can be spectacular in a game. Just getting the ball out, beating their backs and with luck getting it out to our fastest runner on the wing, who can fly over for a try. That's the theory anyway.'

'So what position do you think he'll get me to play?' asked Eoin.

'I don't know, you'd make a pretty good full-back, but with your size and good hands you'd be a good centre too. Maybe even an out-half when you get the hang of it.'

Eoin yawned. 'Sorry, I'm not yawning at you. It's just been a long day.'

'Me too,' said Alan, 'I'm whacked.'

Eoin eventually hopped into bed before the rest of his room-mates had even come back upstairs. He opened the first page of the little green book and read the title once again. Before he had even got to the word 'Finn' his eyes were shut and his first school day was over.

CHAPTER 6

Eoin settled in easily to life at Castlerock College. He found the lessons interesting – except Maths, which he had never really understood – and his fellow pupils a pretty nice bunch. Alan was his best mate, and was always able to steer him away from trouble.

That usually meant Richie Duffy, whose gang of four acolytes was gaining quite a reputation for bullying the younger classes. Alan had a fantastic knack of knowing exactly where the Duffyites were at any time, and how best to avoid them.

Sadly, rugby practice was becoming the main place where Eoin could not avoid Duffy. The farmyard noises were still to be heard a couple of weeks after Eoin's first day mishap, and still got up his nose.

One Wednesday afternoon Eoin was tying up his boots when Duffy strolled into the changing room.

'Ah, it's Farmer Madden,' he sneered. 'Shouldn't you

be wearing wellies?'

Eoin remembered Alan's advice and ignored him.

'Oh, I forgot you haven't mastered the English language yet. Well just you remember that Richie Duffy has more rugby talent than any of your so-called "illustrious family", no matter what that old fool says,' said Richie before he turned on his heel and left.

Eoin seethed, but bit his lip before he, too, jogged out to the field.

'Right, class,' announced Bandy Carey, 'I'm going to mix the backs from the As and Bs for this exercise, and I'll bring in Madden at full-back on the orange team. Who's the B team full-back … oh yes, Sugrue. You head over to the back pitch with the Cs.'

There was an awkward silence before Sugrue – one of Duffy's disciples – trotted away. Richie Duffy stared at Eoin as if the new boy had personally insulted his grandmother.

The practice went quickly, with Eoin slotting nicely into the more skilful backline. He was quick enough to dodge most of the tackles that came in, but found it harder to make his own attempts at stopping the opposition.

As the players trudged off after the session Eoin heard muttering behind him.

'Farmer Boy, don't you *ever* do that again,' hissed Duffy.

Eoin kept walking, ignoring the bully.

'I'm talking to you,' hissed Duffy.

'And I'm ignoring you, so what's the problem?' shot back Eoin.

The rest of the players laughed, which took Duffy by surprise. He opened his mouth to say something but couldn't think of anything clever. He turned and stormed off, thunder-faced.

Later that evening Eoin and Alan were lounging around the dormitory. Eoin was telling him about his quick reply and how, although he enjoyed it at the time, he was worried that Duffy would now make things awkward for him.

'Look,' said Alan, 'That lad has run this place for too long. You standing up to him today showed the other guys that he can be taken on.'

'Yeah, so I'm going to be the big martyr so Sixth Form can have an easier life. Thanks a bundle,' sighed Eoin.

'Cheer up buddy, let's get going on the next lesson in Rugby University.

'It's probably time you learned about the point scoring system and how the game moves,' said Alan. 'There's two basic ways to score – tipping the ball down behind the other team's line is called a try, and that's worth five points. Sometimes the referee will penalise a defending team who stop the opposition scoring illegally by awarding a penalty try.

'The other way of scoring is by kicking the ball over the crossbar between the posts. After you score a try you get a chance to add two extra points by kicking a conversion.

'You can take this wherever you like on a line drawn straight back from where the ball was touched down. If you score in the corner you'd go right back near to the twenty-two to get a good angle to kick the conversion. That's why you sometimes see a try-scorer running around as near as he can to the posts before he touches down. He does that to help the kicker.'

'Hah, I wondered about that. I saw Brian O'Driscoll do that on the TV last year. Makes sense.'

'So there's two points for a conversion,' said Alan, 'And you get three points for a penalty kick.'

'There seems to be loads of things you get penalties for,' said Eoin.

'Well, it seems like that, but there are a few things that come up all the time, like not staying on your feet in a ruck, not releasing the ball in a ruck, high tackle, offside ...

'I'll come back to that another day. Anyway, the kicker can get three points if he scores so they can really add up for a team. The last way of scoring is the dropped goal. Sometimes if you're on the attack and you just can't break through the defence for a try, it can be better to just take your points. It's three points for a drop, so it's not to be sneezed at. The attack will usually prepare for it at a scrum, by having the out-half move back to give himself a better chance of getting the kick away. The scrum half will get the ball back as fast as he can.'

Eoin nodded.

'The out-half has to take the ball cleanly, steady himself, drop the ball so it hits the ground, and as soon as it does so he has to kick it high and straight between the posts. It's a brilliant skill and can be amazing to watch,' went on Alan. 'If a team is on the attack in the last few seconds of a match – and are only a couple of points behind – it will try to work the play into a position as near as it can to the posts before it sets up a drop.'

'I'm glad I have the easy job at the back then,' joked Eoin.

'I wouldn't speak too soon,' said Alan, 'I'd say Bandy was licking his lips that time you did the GAA thing. You should practice drop-kicking. You never know when you'll need it.'

CHAPTER 7

The next morning Eoin, Alan and Rory walked across to their classroom together. They noticed a huddle around the notice board just inside the door, and the crowd parted as Eoin arrived. News had obviously spread of his spat with Richie Duffy.

'Woo hoo,' said Alan, 'We're all back on the 13Cs for the first game on Saturday.'

Eoin smiled, seeing his name written beside the words 'full-back' for the first time.

Alan was on the right wing and Rory was scrum-half.

The next two days passed in a blur for Eoin, and he concentrated hard at practice, terrified he would make a big mistake.

Alan continued his training course, explaining the shape of a rugby pitch and what all the lines were for.

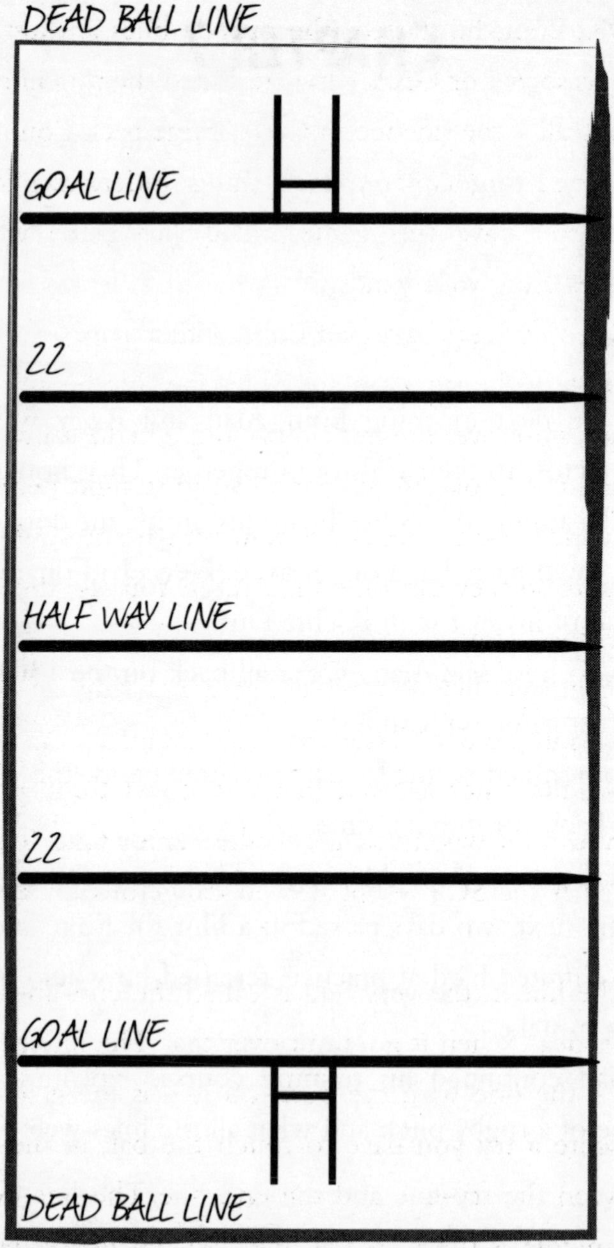

DEAD BALL LINE

GOAL LINE

22

HALF WAY LINE

22

GOAL LINE

DEAD BALL LINE

'OK, Eoin,' he started, 'the outside lines are just the same as soccer or GAA – they're called the touchline.'

'We call it the sideline in GAA,' came back Eoin.

'Sorry, I forgot that you do things differently down there. You have this game called "*foot*-ball", which involves using your hands…'

'Get on with it!' snapped Eoin, with a grin.

'Anyway, the sidelines are along the side here. If the ball goes out over them it's a line-out. The forwards line up and the hooker throws the ball in straight between them. He'll use a code to tell his team who he's going to throw to so they can time their jump. You saw the guys practising them yesterday.'

'Yeah, but they weren't doing that lifting up thing they do in the Six Nations,' quizzed Eoin.

'No, that's not allowed in our rugby. I think you're allowed do it when you get to the Senior Cup Team – *we* call it the SCT – but it's too dangerous for Under 13s.'

'The line at the very end is called the end-line. The ball is dead when it goes out over that. The line before that – the one with the posts on it – is the goal-line. To score a try you have to touch the ball in the area between the try-line and the end-line. The line down the middle is the half-way line, and ten metres either side of that is the ten-metre line. When there's a kick off from half-way the ball has to go over that. The other line is between that and the try-line – it's called "the twenty-two" because it's twenty-two metres out from the posts. It's very important for a full back to know where his own twenty-two is.'

'Why's that?' asked Eoin.

'Well, the main thing is that when you kick for touch you have to keep inside that line. It means you kick the ball straight out and the lineout is taken where the ball goes out. If you kick for touch from outside your own twenty-two then you have to ensure the ball bounces before it goes into touch, which is tricky.'

'What happens if it doesn't,' asked Eoin.

'The touch judge runs all the way back to level where you kicked it from and that's where the line-out happens. That can mean you've lost thirty or forty metres,' explained Alan.

'But if you're inside the twenty-two it doesn't matter if it bounces or not,' said Eoin.

'Exactly – you're getting the hang of it,' laughed Alan.

'Fair play Alan, you're fantastic at making it sound so easy. You must have learned the game as a baby?'

'Not exactly, but my dad and big brothers all played it. They were all really good too', he grimaced. 'I'm a bit of a black sheep that way …'

The pair spent another fifteen minutes going back over the pitch markings and what part they played in the game.

'Do you reckon you'll be OK tomorrow?' asked Alan.

'I dunno,' shrugged Eoin, 'I've worked out the positions and roughly know where I need to be for every move or set-piece. I know I need to pass the ball backwards and not kick the ball upfield like I'm brain-dead.'

'Yeah, well, remember there's a limited number of things that can happen at full-back,' explained Alan, 'so concentrate on watching the ball, going for the high-kicks in your area, and passing the ball back as soon as you're tackled. And get yourself in position to tackle *them* when they're on the attack.'

'Yes, coach,' said Eoin, 'and make sure I cover that useless right winger!' before a pillow flew across the dorm in his direction.

He ducked successfully and laughed as Alan scrambled around looking for more ammunition.

With that the room went dark and the cry of 'lights out!' came along the corridor. The young rugby coach and his pupil chuckled as they hit their beds. Tomorrow would tell just how good a coach and student they were.

CHAPTER 8

Saturday morning was cold, as autumn started to turn into winter. The crisp brown and red leaves that were scattered everywhere around the grounds had started to become a slippery mulch. The Castlerock boarders changed into their kit as soon as breakfast was over, and strolled across to join their teammates at the changing rooms.

Mr Carey was studying his clipboard when Eoin and his pals entered.

'Good morning, boys,' he said, 'take a seat there and we'll go through our plans.'

'Who are we playing, sir?' asked Rory.

'St Ignatius College. They're not a bad team,' said Mr Carey. 'Their Junior Cup Team beat ours last year and they have this Australian guy coaching them. They look a little bit bigger than you guys, so let's make sure we keep it simple. Rory, you captain the team today, and the rest of you just remember what we've been doing these past few weeks. You're a good team and I want to see you putting points on the board.'

The fifteen players – and the five miserable-looking replacements who would have to spend the game shivering on the touchline, waiting for the call – headed out to the rugby field where their opponents were waiting.

Carey hadn't been wrong about their relative size – St Ignatius's had at least four players taller than Lofty O'Flynn, Castlerock's so-called 'giant' second row.

'The bigger they are the harder they fall,' said Rory to the pack as they waited for Harry Deacon to kick-off for Castlerock.

Once the ball was lifted into the air, St Ignatius's giants came charging forward and, with a well-drilled move, the first to the ball leapt high and snatched it from the air. The rest of the pack formed a protective group around the catcher and they started to move forwards.

'That's a maul,' said Alan to Eoin, who was a few yards away. 'The guy with the ball is still on his feet – our forwards have to stop him or they'll come straight to our line.'

After about fifteen metres the maul was toppled and the ball fed back to the visiting scrum-half.

He fed it out to his backs and the left winger was

suddenly facing Alan. The Castlerock winger was slow reading the situation and when his opponent turned back inside he was left grasping fresh air.

With the field wide open the St Ignatius winger sprinted for the line, but just as he moved to dive over for a try he was hit with an almighty thump on his right thigh. He toppled sideways, but his attempt to throw the ball back was haywire and it flew into touch.

'Thanks Eoin,' puffed Alan, as he raced past the full-back into his position. 'That was some tackle.'

From the line-out Castlerock scrambled back the ball and out-half Harry Deacon cleared it up-field.

Eoin was getting warmed up now and had enjoyed making the tackle, although his shoulder blades were starting to smart a bit.

Once play settled down it seemed that the visitors' pack wasn't as formidable as it looked, although they continued to win plenty of the line-outs.

Mr Carey was refereeing, and he was hard on his own team's mistakes, awarding several penalties against Castlerock within kicking range. Luckily the visitors' kicker was hopeless with anything that wasn't straight in front of the posts and he scored just two out of six, giving his team a narrow 6-3 lead at half time.

St Ignatius changed their kicker after the break, bringing on a small, wiry fellow who was stuck out on the wing. He was a poor handler and missed several tackles, but he was a gifted goal-kicker. With ten minutes left he had single handedly extended his team's lead to 15–3 with three penalty goals from three attempts.

Castlerock were starting to flag, but at a break in play Rory gathered the team around him.

'Come on 'Rock, we can do this,' said the little scrum-half. Those big guys are knackered now. We can push them around the park and get back in this game. No kicking for touch – they're hammering us in the line-outs – so let's try to get the ball out to the backs and get some moves going.'

From the next scrum, just inside St Ignatius's half, the ball was duly worked back to Rory, who fed Harry. The out-half shrugged off two tackles as he made his way into the 22. He was floored by the full-back, but got the ball off to Alan who sprinted as hard as he could for the corner.

Just before he reached the flag he saw one of the St Ignatius ogres coming towards him at speed. He immediately turned back inside and slipped the ball to Eoin who was right on his shoulder.

With a powerful dive Castlerock's newest star flew over the goal-line for the first try of his short rugby career.

Eoin picked himself up to see Mr Carey's beaming grin and Rory slapping him on the back. 'Great try, Madden,' said the scrum-half as the conversion sailed over the bar to make it 15–10, 'now let's get back quickly and try to win this.'

Rory was proved right about the St Ignatius pack, which seemed to have run out of steam. Scrum after scrum was won before Castlerock worked themselves into a strong position with two minutes left.

Disastrously, Rory's pass out to Harry fell short and went to ground, where the visitors' flanker pounced on the ball. The ruck led to the ball coming back to St Ignatius and an attack was on. Their out-half danced through three tackles before he turned to spin a long pass out to the outside centre.

Eoin spotted what the out-half was trying to do and sprinted like a greyhound between the St Ignatius's backs, snapping the ball out of the air.

Stunned, the visitors' backs turned and chased hard as Eoin headed for their line. With only the full back to beat, Eoin veered out to the right.

As he raced towards the line he realised he was heading for the corner. Remembering what Alan had taught him about making the kicker's job easier, he took one step back to his left and completely wrong-footed the full back, who slipped and fell over.

It was then a simple job of touching the ball down under the posts which Eoin did without fuss. He turned to see fourteen boys racing towards him with faces full of delight.

'Fantastic try, Eoin …'

'Unbelievable …'

'What a side-step …'

It was all a blur as he walked back to half-way and watched Harry smack over the winning conversion.

Mr Carey's blast on the whistle was followed by another long one to signal the game was over.

After Rory called for three cheers for St Ignatius, and both teams shook hands, the entire Castlerock team descended once again on Eoin for more congratulations.

Mr Carey came over to talk to them and was full of praise for everyone on the team who had played their part in the amazing fight-back. He grinned at Eoin, but didn't add to the flood of praise that was already making the full-back feel uncomfortable.

As the team walked off, Mr Finn waved to Eoin as he passed.

'The green book must be doing you some good,' he called.

Eoin blushed.

'It is,' he lied, 'I really enjoyed it.'

'What book?' asked Alan, as they walked on.

'Mr Finn's old rugby coaching book. Bandy gave it to me,' explained Eoin. 'I haven't even opened it.'

'Well there's your weekend gone,' laughed Alan. 'We have him first thing Monday morning. He'll probably want to go over it page by page with you now!'

CHAPTER 9

Eoin was terrified of upsetting Mr Finn and so spent all Saturday evening lying on his bed reading his ancient coaching book.

It wasn't as bad as he expected, as Mr Finn had quite a good sense of humour and used lots of little stories to help make a point. The photos were a bit weird looking, with old rugby stars wearing plain-coloured jerseys that looked like they were made out of thick sackcloth.

At the very end of the book there was a picture of Mr Finn in his playing days standing beside a taller man. The History teacher had a moustache that made Eoin smile. The other man was sort of familiar, but Eoin still got a shock when he read the caption.

'Andy Finn and "Dixie" Madden, a fine half-back partnership.'

It was the first time he had seen a photograph of his grandfather in his youth and it was noticeable how he had obviously inherited his looks. Eoin closed the book and lay back on the pillow. There was much of the past that he didn't know about and he was particularly puzzled at the mystery of his grandfather's rugby career.

He glanced at his watch and hopped off the bed. It was a quarter to nine, just time for a quick phone call home to his mum and dad.

He walked quickly down the stairs to the common room where one of the fifth year boys was on the phone. He went on and on, and Eoin kept glancing at his watch. At two minutes to nine he hung up, smirking at the younger boy as he walked away.

Eoin grabbed the receiver and hurriedly punched the number into the phone. His mum answered and sounded delighted to hear from him.

'It's great to talk to you, Eoin,' said his Mum, 'but it's not like you to ring on a Saturday night. I hope you're all right?'

'I'm fine, Mum, is Dad there?' he asked.

'Why, is there something wrong?' she asked.

'No, I just need to ask him something.'

Eoin's father came on the line.

'How are you, son?' he asked, sounding slightly concerned.

'I'm fine, Dad,' said Eoin, 'I've just been thinking

about Grandad and was wondering why he never kept up playing rugby. They all go on about him up here and even the kids seem to know more about him than I do.'

'Well …' said Dad, hesitantly, 'I'm not sure I can go into that now. Grandad is a very private man …'

With that, one of the teachers came around the corner blowing a whistle.

'Nine o'clock, bed time for all juniors!' he bellowed. 'You! Hang up that call,' he said, pointing at Eoin.

'OK, Dad, I've got to go,' said Eoin, 'talk to you soon.'

He replaced the receiver in its cradle and raced back up the stairs. He barely had time to change into his pyjamas when the lights went out.

'Good night, guys,' he called out, but his room-mates were already asleep.

CHAPTER 10

Alan was proved right about Mr Finn and his History class on Monday. He spent most of the lesson talking about old-time rugby and how different a game it was then. He explained that when he first played it was just three points for a try, before it was increased to four in 1971 and five in 1991.

Back then there was not as much emphasis on fitness and coaching, and players weren't paid to play.

'It was amazing,' he explained. 'Fellows would spend all week working in a bank or a coal-mine and then on Saturday they would turn up and play for their country. They just didn't have the time to practise and train as much as modern players. But it was much more fun ...'

'Sir,' said Charlie Johnston, who played No.8 on the 13As. 'Sir, were you a good player back then?'

'No, no, no, not at all,' said Mr Finn. 'I was a very limited scrum-half, but I played on a very good team, and had a world-class out-half alongside me.'

Eoin blushed, already aware which way the conversation was going.

'Richard Madden and I formed a half-back partnership when we were your age, boys, and kept it going for more than a decade. We won the Schools Junior Cup, Schools Senior Cup and then the Leinster Senior Cup with the old boys' club. I still consider myself fortunate to have achieved what I did in the game. The sport of rugby has given me immense pleasure over the years and I enjoy nothing more than watching young men such as yourselves learning to have the same fun. Some of you may even be good enough to become professional players in the future, but I do hope you remember that at its heart this is still a pastime, a fabulous way of enjoying yourself with your friends.'

Eoin thought about what Mr Finn had said as he walked to his next class. He met Rory on the way.

'Hey, Madden, Mr Carey was obviously impressed with the two of us on Saturday. We've both been promoted to the 13Bs for the game on Wednesday!'

Eoin was stunned, and a little upset by the news. All his pals were on the 13Cs, and he felt he wasn't nearly good enough to be moving up after just one game.

By Wednesday he was deeply unhappy. To make matters worse, Alan hadn't reacted at all well to the news.

'We've a good thing going on the Cs,' he complained, 'can't you just tell Bandy you don't want to play Bs?'

'Ah come on, where would that get me?' answered Eoin, 'I'd be hammered for that. No way would he let me.'

Alan's rugby lessons came to an abrupt halt and the two only exchanged words when they had to.

As kick-off time approached Eoin was sitting in the Bs' dressing room waiting for Mr Carey or Mr Maguire to come in and give the team talk. He looked around at his new team-mates and realised they were just as nervous as he was. If he remembered the coach's words he'd be fine.

Suddenly, in strode Mr Carey, looking quite flustered. 'Right,' he said, 'who plays centre on this team?'

Two boys put their hands up.

'McCann ... Anderson ...' he muttered, before his eyes travelled along the benches that ran around three of the walls.

His eyes stopped when they reached Eoin.

'Madden,' he said. 'That Redmond lad has just gone over on his ankle in the warm-up. We're short a centre on the As. Come with me.'

Eoin's face fell. He wanted to say 'But, sir—' but his

mouth was so dry he could barely get a squeak out. He stood up and followed the coach out the door.

Out on the field the 13As were gathered around a boy who was lying on the ground sobbing. He was clearly in pain and Miss O'Dea, the school nurse, was wrapping a bandage around his ankle.

As Eoin came towards them, Richie Duffy looked up and glared at him.

'Right, team, gather round,' said Mr Carey, 'This is Eoin Madden, he's new this year, but he'll do a good job for us today. He'll slot in at full back and Billy Ryan can move to outside centre. Now let's get warmed up again. Quickly!'

Mr Carey took Eoin aside.

'Right, Eoin, I want you to keep things very simple today. Just concentrate on collecting the high balls and making your tackles. I don't want you coming through looking for interceptions – this is a higher-level rugby and they'll punish any mistakes you make. But enjoy yourself, and learn.'

To enjoy himself was the last thing Eoin expected from the game, and he was proved correct. He made some tackles, but missed a couple too and on a couple of occasions the opposition players crashed right through his grasp.

Castlerock escaped with a 20-20 draw, but Eoin was directly to blame for their opponents' final, equalising try. Richie Duffy was quick to remind him of the missed tackle as the teams walked off at the end.

'You are so rubbish, Madden. I don't expect we'll see you on this team again,' he muttered.

Eoin walked away, wishing Alan and Rory were there to give him support. He bit his lip, not sure whether a reply to Duffy was a good idea, but certain that to show even a single tear would destroy his name in the school.

CHAPTER 11

It seemed to Eoin as if life couldn't get much worse.

'Thirty-two nil. And we were lucky to get nil,' moaned Alan in the dormitory that night, 'thanks a bunch, buddy'.

'Ah come on, Alan, I had no choice. And even if I played for the Cs I wouldn't have made much difference, surely?' Eoin replied.

Alan shrugged, turned his back on him, and returned to sharing his woes with Mighty the Mouse.

The guys on the 13Bs were a bit miffed, too, at his brief appearance in their dressing room, while the 13As blamed that missed tackle for costing them their 100 per cent record.

All in all, it was a pretty awful couple of days for Eoin.

The double period of History on Friday wasn't until after lunch, which was why everyone was surprised when Mr Finn poked his head around the door before the first class that morning.

'Gentlemen,' he announced, 'We will have a special excursion this afternoon. We will meet at the front of the school at 1.15pm. Please be punctual or we will be forced to leave you behind for a triple period of Mathematics.'

And with that, he was gone.

There was much speculation about the destination of the trip, with most of the boys expecting a return visit to Kilmainham Gaol or the National Museum.

'It'll be the only time the boggers will get to see their Mummies this side of Christmas,' sneered Richie Duffy.

But they were all wrong.

The bus drove towards the city, but after a short journey they turned into a leafy road and crossed the Dart tracks. Everyone stared out the windows at the colossal structure overhead.

As they arrived, Mr Finn stood up at the front of the bus.

'Gentlemen, welcome to Lansdowne Road, or the Aviva Stadium as it is now called. This fine structure took four years to build and was opened in 2010. It replaced the old rugby ground which holds so many memories for me, and of course for the school.

'We will be having a tour of the stadium and hearing something of its extraordinary history. You are representing your school, so I expect you gentlemen to be on your best behaviour and to respect the places we visit and the people we meet.'

The group stepped down from the bus on Lansdowne Road and went through the double glass doors to the stadium foyer.

A friendly young woman brought them through the turnstile into a long, high tunnel. 'This tunnel goes right around the ground. We need it so big to get buses and ambulances right into the stadium,' she explained.

She led the boys up a passageway into a brightly-lit area with huge murals showing great footballers and rugby players of the past.

'This is the players' tunnel, where they run out onto the pitch. They come out of their dressing rooms, on either side here, when it's near kick-off time.'

Eoin noticed how some of the guys were wide-eyed with wonderment, one or two even practising their strut along the tunnel, lost in some long-held dream that they might take that same walk some day when the stadium was full.

There was none of that nonsense in Eoin's head, just a growing boredom and the growing realisation that he probably didn't like rugby at all.

'Keep up, Mr Madden,' said Mr Finn, 'We're going into the players' area now. It's very impressive.'

The group walked into the home dressing room and took a seat on the long benches around the walls. The guide showed the boys the DVD screen where last minute tactics could be explained, and they were suitably impressed by the enormous shower and bathing area.

'There were five shower heads between the team when I last played here,' smiled Mr Finn, 'And only two of them produced warm water.'

The guide showed them into another part of the players' area – a huge room with a floor covered in artificial grass. 'This is where players can practise last minute line-out calls, or even do some kicking,' she explained.

Even Mr Finn's eyes widened at this extraordinary facility.

'What will they think of next?' he wondered aloud.

The boys took it in turn to squeeze through the narrow door into the warm-up room and, as Eoin had been in the first group, he wandered around outside waiting for the rest of the party to finish.

He realised that he hadn't exchanged a single word with anyone on the trip, as his only current friend, Rory, was back at school with a high temperature.

He rambled down a corridor looking for the bath-room, but after taking a couple of turns he realised all the doors looked the same and he wasn't sure which way to go next. He tried a couple of the doorknobs, but the rooms were locked.

Eoin noticed the last door on the corridor had a white square on the door with a red cross in the middle, which he worked out was the First Aid room.

He tried the handle and the door opened, and he went straight to the lavatory. As he washed his hands he heard a noise behind him and turned quickly.

Sitting on the treatment table was a young man wear-ing a black, red and yellow hooped jersey and black shorts. He was holding his head in his hands and what Eoin could see of his face looked very pale.

'Hello, are you OK?' asked Eoin.

The man lifted his head and stared at Eoin.

'Who are you?' he asked.

'I'm Eoin. I'm here on a school tour and just got lost. Are you injured?'

'I suppose you could say that. I got a knock to my head a while ago. It still hurts. What school are you from?'

'Castlerock,' said Eoin.

'Ahhh, Castlerock,' said the man, 'Had a few good games against them in my school days. Good team, they won everything for years.'

Eh? He must be confused after that knock on the head, thought Eoin.

'Where are you from?' asked the man.

'Ormondstown,' said Eoin, 'It's in Tipper—'

'I know exactly where it is,' he replied, 'Sure amn't I from Clonmel myself? I thought I recognised your accent. Do you play rugby up in Castlerock yourself?'

'I do, but I'm not sure I like it very much. I've just started and they promoted me from the Cs to the As after one game. I haven't a clue what's going on half the time and when I do something wrong everyone blames me.'

'Ah sure, didn't the same happen to me when I first came up to school. I had a brother who was pretty good – he went on to play for Ireland – and everyone thought I was going to be a natural. I never even saw a game of rugby down home in Clonmel before I was picked on the school team. They made a right fool of me.'

'How did you get around it?' asked Eoin.

'I worked at it, learned everything I could about the game and practised on my own whenever I could.'

'I'm not sure I want to go through all that...' started Eoin.

'Listen,' said the man, 'Just you remember that rugby

is a great game for young lads. It will help you get fit and stay fit, and it teaches you all sorts of things about teamwork and co-operation. It suits all shapes and sizes and a friend you make on the rugby pitch will be a friend for life.'

The pair talked for a few minutes about a few of the things Eoin found tricky, including the best way to make a tackle.

Eoin suddenly realised he had been there for twenty minutes and the teachers would be looking for him.

'I've got to go,' he said, 'thanks for the tips.'

'No bother at all,' said the man, 'if you need any more help I'm usually around here somewhere. Do call back and say hello. By the way, my name's Brian.'

Eoin trotted up the corridor and back through the dressing rooms. He arrived back in the tunnel just as the Castlerock group came back in from the pitch.

'Mr Madden, did you run ahead?' asked Mr Finn. 'I didn't see you out in the arena.'

'No sir, I was tagging along,' said Eoin. 'I had a stone in my shoe, maybe you didn't see me because I was bending down?' he suggested.

The tour wound up and the boys all climbed back into the bus. Mr Finn came down the aisle and sat in beside Eoin for a minute.

'Is everything all right?' he asked, 'You seem in bad form.'

'No sir, I'll be fine,' muttered Eoin.

The teacher stood up, nodded, and walked away, leaving Eoin alone with confused thoughts about whether he really disliked rugby or not. He thought about Brian and his sensible advice.

He'd give it another go.

CHAPTER 12

After his stinker for the As, Eoin was allowed drop back to the Bs for the next couple of games. He started to enjoy playing again, and found the Bs much more fun than the As – who were too serious – and the Cs – who were just too hopeless. After Eoin's remarkable contribution to the win over St Ignatius's, the Cs lost their next seven games, usually by a wide margin.

Alan eventually realised the problem was not that Eoin wasn't playing, and that even if it was, he could hardly be blamed for it. The pair made up over a packet of peanuts in the dorm one night.

'I'm sorry I've been such a prat,' said Alan. 'I was just a bit jealous that you were getting on the Bs so quickly. I've been playing for years and I've never got a sniff.'

Eoin smiled. Alan really loved his rugby, but just hadn't got the co-ordination to ever become any good at it. He wished he could switch their abilities around, but knew that wasn't going to happen.

'I'll try to hammer the Bs winger in the warm-up – maybe Carey will sub you up then?' he joked.

'Carey would sooner play the Bs prop on the wing than move me up. I'm stuck with the Cs forever,' said Alan, gloomily.

'We should organise a couple of training sessions ourselves on one of the out-of-the-way pitches,' said Eoin, 'Brian said he used to practise on his own.'

'Who's Brian?' asked Alan.

'Just this guy I met in the Aviva,' said Eoin.

'Where in the Aviva?' asked Alan.

'In the First Aid room. I got a bit lost looking for the loo,' explained Eoin.

'You're lucky Finn didn't catch you, they go mad if you go off on your own like that,' said Alan. 'Anyway, let's have a look at trying a few things, it can't be any worse than it is.'

On Sunday morning all the boarders were expected at the college chapel for nine o'clock mass. Eoin and Alan joined the service, with their tracksuits and boots stuffed in backpacks hidden under the benches.

As mass ended, they scarpered around the side of the chapel, terrified that they would be seen. There was nothing wrong with what they were planning, but if it got out it would only provide more ammunition for Duffy and his cronies.

When the coast was clear they wandered down through the bushes and undergrowth to a quiet corner of the school grounds. The tall trees blocked the view of the school so the pair could practise in peace.

'How about we start with me trying to tackle you, and you trying to dodge me,' said Eoin. 'We're both weak at those things.'

Eoin had read through Mr Finn's book the night before and had picked up some insights into the art of tackling. Mr Finn made the point that tackling was not about physical power – it was about technique more than anything, with mental strength being just as important as physical strength.

Alan picked up the ball and, standing twenty yards away, started to run towards Eoin. Alan took a couple of steps to his right, trying to run past Eoin, who dived headlong at Alan's feet.

'Ouch,' roared Eoin, as Alan's heels clattered into his face. The winger toppled over, but Eoin was left writhing on the ground in agony.

'Too low,' said Alan. 'You've got to aim for the middle of my thigh – use the end of a player's shorts as the target.'

'So it's your fault, then,' joked Eoin, 'Wearing that tracksuit confused me!'

'You have to get nearer to the player too,' said Alan, 'You should be trying to hit with your shoulder, not your hands and arms.'

They practised for twenty minutes before Eoin got the hang of it. They then took turns playing the other's role, which was less successful as Eoin was always able to avoid Alan's tackle.

To finish off their session they stood forty yards apart and kicked the ball high in the air towards the other. Eoin's gaelic football skills meant he was always quick to reach for the ball and take it cleanly. Alan was less successful, but started to develop a technique of getting underneath the ball and having his arms ready to hug it to his chest.

'Let's call it a day,' said Alan, as he dropped the ball for the umpteenth time. 'The ball's getting slippery with all these wet leaves. That was good fun though.'

They walked back to the school, working out plans for their Sunday afternoon. Arsenal on the TV seemed the best bet.

As they reached the door, Miss O'Dea came out, looking flustered.

'Eoin Madden, where have you been? We've been

looking for you everywhere,' she told him.

'Why, Miss, what's wrong?'

'Your father has rung the school four times this morning. Come with me, you can use the staff room telephone to call him back.'

Eoin dashed up the steps in pursuit of Miss O'Dea, leaving Alan standing holding the ball.

'Dad?' he asked, as the phone was answered in Ormondstown.

'Oh, Eoin, thank God, we were just about to leave. Where have you been?'

'I've been out playing rugby with Alan. What's wrong?'

'It's Grandad, he's had a turn. The ambulance came for him. They've taken him to Dublin. We'll collect you at three o'clock.'

CHAPTER 13

Eoin was terrified. He knew his grandad hadn't been in good health for a while, but he had always been a huge part of his life and Eoin couldn't bear to think of what it would be like without him.

He thanked Miss O'Dea and as he walked out the door of the staff room he bumped into Mr Finn.

'Sir, I've had some bad news about Grandad.'

'Dixie ...' gasped the teacher, his face falling.

'He's been taken to hospital up in Dublin, sir. I'm not sure what's wrong with him, but my parents are collecting me at three o'clock.'

'I'm very sorry to hear that, Eoin,' said Mr Finn, 'please give him my very best wishes. And do come and tell me the news when you return to the school.'

Eoin took his time walking back to the dormitory.

Alan had filled in Kevin, Anton, Fiachra and Rory on the drama and they were all silent when Eoin arrived in the room.

He stopped at the door once again, gently running his fingers along the plaque carrying the name of the dormitory.

'It's Grandad,' he said. 'I'll be going to the hospital at three. Hopefully he'll be fine.'

The boys looked shocked, even a little upset, and Fiachra seemed to avoiding his stare. But then Eoin remembered that the name 'Dixie Madden' still meant a lot to these lads who'd never even met his grandad.

'He's a tough old guy,' he said, unconvincingly.

Eoin didn't bother going down for lunch, even though he was hungry after the morning's run-out.

He lay on the bed, going through all the times he had with his grandad, but trying hard not to think that there mightn't be any more. Grandad never missed a school sports day, or a gaelic match, or even that stupid school play when Eoin had to dress up as a giant chicken. And everything Eoin had learned about nature and wildlife came on those regular Sunday morning walks between mass and his mother's roast lunch.

He thought, too, of the mystery of Dixie's rugby career and grew angry with himself that he hadn't talked to his grandfather about it back home in Ormondstown.

Alan and Rory came up to the dorm after Sunday

lunch, sneaking in a couple of bread rolls for Eoin.

'Thanks guys,' he said, as he munched into the crusty bread. 'I couldn't face the rest of the school.'

'I don't blame you,' said Rory, 'Richie Duffy was asking where you were. I told him you were off having a trial for Leinster Under 13s!'

'Ha, ha,' chuckled Eoin, before realising Duffy would surely find out the truth and make his life even more difficult.

'You better hurry up with those,' said Alan, 'it's five to three.'

Eoin grabbed his hoodie and waved farewell to his pals as he dashed off, continuing to chew the rolls.

Outside he waited at the top of the long driveway until he saw the silver car come through the gates. He set off at a trot down the drive, meeting the car just as it came around a bend.

'God, Eoin, you gave me a fright,' said his dad.

'That makes two of us,' said Eoin, 'What's wrong with Grandad?'

'He had a bit of a turn, something to do with his heart,' said Dad, 'I just rang the hospital and he's already settled in. We'll go straight there now.'

'Hi, Mum,' said Eoin, as he hopped into the back seat of the car.

'You look like you've lost weight, are you eating properly?' she asked.

'Yeah, the food's not too bad. I missed lunch, though, any chance we can grab a burger on the way?'

Eoin sat munching in the waiting room as his dad talked to the doctors. Grandad was asleep and wouldn't be able to see anyone until the morning, but they could go in and look at him for a moment.

Eoin held his mother's hand as they walked into the darkened room with lots of machines with blinking lights and tubes.

He whispered, 'Hi Dixie, make sure you hang in there. We've a lot to talk about it,' so quietly that even his mum couldn't hear him.

The family sat around the waiting room for an hour, just chatting over things and swopping the news from school and home. Despite the circumstances, the afternoon cheered up Eoin greatly and he had a smile on his face as he hugged his mum goodbye outside the school.

He called by the staff common room to fill Mr Finn in on the news and the teacher thanked him.

As Eoin turned to leave, he hesitated for a moment, before turning back to face the teacher.

'Mr Finn. Why did Grandad not play for Ireland if he was as good as everyone says he was?'

'Oh, Eoin, you poor lad,' said the old man slowly, his eyes looking as sad as Eoin had ever seen on anyone. 'That's a story that only Dixie himself can tell you. Do you know, I think about him almost every day and every time I wince with regret and pain. But I'm sorry, it would be quite wrong of me to tell you that story. Now, off to the dorm with you, it's coming up to lights out.'

Eoin jogged up the stairs and kept moving quickly through the dormitory. He made it plain to his room-mates that he wasn't in a chatty mood and so they steered well clear of him.

Sleep didn't come easy, but by the time it did Eoin's pillow was soaked.

CHAPTER 14

Dixie's health improved, and Eoin's parents were able to go home to Tipperary after a week or so. Eoin enjoyed seeing his parents: each day they collected him after homework, brought him out for a meal and then took him down to visit the hospital.

The three of them sat with Dixie for half an hour each evening, keeping him amused with little stories of life back home. As they got up to leave one night, he called Eoin back for a quiet word.

'I hear you're getting on well at the rugby. It must be hard for you to take it up when everything else is so new to you too. But stick at it, Eoin; it's the most fantastic fun. When I look back on my life I reckon my rugby days were the happiest of all ...'

'I'm doing OK,' said Eoin, 'but I'm still struggling with a lot of things.'

'Well, you must tell me about them next time. Is Andy

Finn still coaching there?'

'No,' said Eoin, 'He teaches me History, but he's not involved with rugby any more. He told me he used to play with you.' He paused for a moment. 'Can I ask you a question, Grandad?' he said.

The old man stopped and looked into Eoin's eyes.

'I know what you're going to ask me, and I'm afraid I'm not going to answer you now. It would be very upsetting to go over it all again, and I don't have my strength. But I'll tell you what. The first Six Nations game of the year is in February. If I'm out and about I'll bring you to that game and we'll have a great day out. And I'll tell you the whole story of my rugby career, if it's not too boring ...'

Eoin stood up and smiled.

'That would be brilliant, Grandad, I hope you get better really soon.'

Back on the Bs, a grudge match against the B team of their local rival St Paschal's turned into a landslide win for Castlerock, with Eoin clearly the star player. Even still, it was quite a shock for Eoin when he heard the news.

'You're on the As,' blurted Rory as he ran up the corridor early one morning. 'At inside centre!'

Eoin went white. 'Oh no ...' he said.

'Whaaaat?' said Rory, 'that's a fantastic honour! You only took the game up three months ago and here you are on the Castlerock first fifteen for the first round of the Under 13 Cup. That's unheard of!'

Eoin couldn't share in Rory's delight, and as he saw Alan's face he knew that his friend understood too.

'Hang on, Rory,' said Alan, 'Flanagan plays inside centre for the As, and he's Duffy's best mate, they're not going to be delighted about him being dropped.'

'And I'm sure Richie won't be too keen on having me standing next to him,' grumbled Eoin.

Alan was right. Richie Duffy's face was the colour of a Welsh jersey when he saw Eoin enter the classroom.

The teacher was already writing on the blackboard, so Duffy couldn't say anything aloud. But Eoin got his message quite clearly when the class bully pointed to the side of his neck and drew his finger across slowly to the other side.

The day passed far too slowly for Eoin's liking, and more than once a teacher had to disturb him from his daydream as he tried to work out a way to get out of the mess. He wasn't afraid of Duffy really, but he was only new to rugby and had so much more to learn about the game. Playing 'A' team cup rugby for the school was a serious responsibility in Castlerock.

Eoin's dad rang that evening.

'Eoin, what do you say about going to see Munster play Leinster at the Aviva? It's on Friday night and I can pick you up from school.'

'That would be great, Dad, but won't I have to be back before nine o'clock? I have a big match on Saturday morning.'

'Go and ask Mr Finn for permission, I'm sure he'll be fine with it.'

Mr Finn was indeed fine, extending Eoin's curfew to ten o'clock with a special pass. He asked how Eoin's grandfather was feeling and again asked him to pass on his best wishes.

'It's been too long since I saw Dixie, do you think he'd like if I came to visit?'

Eoin wasn't sure, but told Mr Finn that he'd ask his dad.

CHAPTER 15

Friday arrived, and Eoin was pretty excited about getting to see his first big match. His dad called for him at 4.30pm and they made a quick detour to visit Grandad in hospital.

There were fewer wires around his bed now, and he was in a bright, sunny room with three other men.

'So you're off to Lansdowne, Eoin,' said Dixie, 'or The Viva I believe they call it now.'

'The *A*-viva, Grandad,' laughed Eoin. 'I was there on a school tour a while back, it's an amazing place.'

'It surely is,' said Grandad, 'I saw some amazing players there in my youth – have you ever heard of Jackie Kyle? What an out-half he was. Mike Gibson, Willie John McBride, ah a magical place it was, magical.'

The old man reached over to his locker and produced a fifty euro note.

'Take this, Kevin,' he said to Eoin's dad, handing over

the money, 'and buy the lad a Munster jersey. They'll need all the support they can get tonight.'

'Thanks so much, Grandad,' said a delighted Eoin. 'I promise I'll roar them on loud enough for the two of us!'

After a quick detour to the stadium shop to buy the jersey, the Madden father and son took their seats high in the West Stand.

They enjoyed the pre-match atmosphere and Eoin read the programme avidly, picking up more and more details for the rugby database in his brain that Alan had started to fill.

With twenty minutes to kick-off Eoin turned to his dad.

'I'm starving! Do you fancy a hot dog?'

'No, I'm fine,' said his father, 'Have you enough money?'

'I've a bit of change from the jersey, and I'm famished. I won't be long.'

Eoin darted down the steep steps, taking care not to miss his footing. He passed the press box, where the reporters were plugging in their laptops and checking the programme against the names on their team-sheets. *That looks like a nice job*, he thought.

Behind the stand was a large area with souvenir stalls,

vending machines and fast food restaurants. Eoin asked a nice girl for a hot dog, and blushed when she smiled at him as she handed him the change.

He looked at his watch as he munched the sausage, and took in his surroundings. The place was thronged with blue shirts, but there were a good number of red ones too.

'It's bogger!' came a cry from behind him.

He turned to see Richie Duffy and Ollie Flanagan pointing at him. The pair were wearing blue Leinster jerseys and the two men with them, presumably their fathers, wore the same, in XXXL sizes.

'That's the culchie who's keeping me off the team,' spat Flanagan.

'Well,' muttered his father, 'I don't expect that will be for much longer. Can't have ... *Munster* men representing Castlerock College at Donnybrook you know.'

Eoin turned away, desperate to escape the mass of blue shirts, and those four in particular.

He ducked around a corner where he found a doorway, which his natural nosiness ensured he opened and entered.

When the floor started to move Eoin got a fright, before he realised he was in some sort of service elevator. He pushed all the buttons and was relieved that no-one was about when the door opened.

Eoin looked around him, seeing a wall completely covered in old team group photographs, which reminded him of the great hall back in Castlerock.

A table was set with a tempting array of hundreds of bite-sized snacks, and Eoin instantly regretted the hot dog he was already digesting.

One side of the room was a glass wall, outside which Eoin could see the floodlights and fans in the opposite grandstand. He realised he was in some sort of VIP area.

'So it's a VIP you are, then?' asked a voice.

Eoin swung around to see Brian who, strangely, was still wearing the black, red and yellow jersey and black shorts.

Eoin pointed to the wall where a group was wearing the same kit. 'Is that your team?' he asked.

'Well, it's one of the teams that came after me,' he said. 'That's the Lansdowne team of 1981. They won the Senior Cup out there to complete a three-in-a-row. Fantastic team, a tough bunch led by a giant of a man from Kerry called Moss Keane.'

Eoin thought Brian looked a bit young to remember that, but let it slide.

'I don't know how I got in here. I'm lost,' he explained.

'Sure you're always getting lost,' laughed Brian. 'Are

you here for the game?'

'Yeah, my dad's upstairs,' explained Eoin.

'How's the rugby going for you,' asked Brian.

'Great ... well, no, terrible really,' said Eoin. 'I've been picked for the A team for the cup match, but none of the players want me to play. The game is in the morning and I'm thinking of going sick.'

'Don't be daft,' said Brian. 'What's the worst that could happen?'

'We could lose, and I could be blamed again,' said Eoin.

'Teams lose all the time, and it's always someone's fault. They'll get over it and so will you. You have a chance here to show what you can do at a higher level than ever before. You have to take it. How have you been playing since I saw you last. Did the tackling improve?' asked Brian.

'It did, actually,' said Eoin, 'I worked out when it's best to dive and where to hit. I made a couple of cracking tackles in the last game.'

'Great, so just keep doing that. Are you playing full-back?'

'No, inside centre. And the out-half hates my guts.'

'Hmmm, that could be tricky,' said Brian. 'Just make sure you're always there to receive the pass, even if it never comes. Now, you better get back to your seat or your dad will be wondering where you are. Good luck tomorrow and don't forget to drop back and say hello.'

Eoin was just about to thank Brian when he heard the door open behind him.

'Who are you?' asked a steward, 'And how did you get in here?'

'I got off the lift at the wrong floor,' explained Eoin.

'Who were you talking to?' asked the steward.

'Just Brian there,' said Eoin, turning to point at the Lansdowne player, but only finding thin air.

'There's no-one there,' said the steward.

Eoin was puzzled. Where could Brian have gone so quickly? He hadn't heard any move from the sliding glass door out into the arena.

'He was here a second ago – he was wearing Lansdowne gear.'

'Well he's not here now,' said the steward, looking at Eoin as if he were mad.

Eoin made his way back to the lift, and up to his seat on the top deck.

His dad was relieved to see him.

'What kept you, I was starting to worry?'

'Oh, I met a couple of school mates. We just got chatting,' he said.

The game had already kicked off and Eoin soon got wrapped up in the excitement. Munster's powerful forwards dominated early on, but as soon as Leinster got the ball back out of the set plays there was a tingle of excitement around the stadium. The home team had a star-studded back line and they waltzed through the Munster tackles time after time.

With just three minutes left Leinster led 24–22 and Eoin could hardly bear to watch.

The Munster forwards were moving slowly up-field, inching the maul towards the Leinster 22. The blue flankers kept charging in, but the men in red held firm. Eventually the maul was felled and the referee awarded Munster a scrum.

The stadium clock showed there was less than a minute left in the game when the ball came back out of the scrum on the Munster side. Eoin noticed that Ronan O'Gara had stepped back a few yards and was wiping his hands on the back of his shorts.

'They're going for a dropped goal,' Eoin said to his dad.

His dad smiled back. 'You seem to know your stuff,' he said.

Sure enough, Tomás O'Leary spun the ball out to the Munster No.10. Time seemed to stand still as he dropped the ball to the ground. In the instant it hit the turf, O'Gara's powerful boot swung hard and smacked into the leather ball.

It flew high into the air, tumbling over on itself like a rabbit scampering away from a hound. The ball reached its peak high above the crowd who, as one, watched as it hovered for a moment before it slowly began its descent.

It fell right between the upright posts, where the referee had run to check the accuracy of the kick. He raised his hand high and blew his whistle.

The clock had already ticked on to '40', so the referee lifted his whistle to his lips once more. Game over: 25-24 to Munster.

Eoin leapt from his seat and hugged his dad.

'That was brilliant,' he said, 'What a game!'

All the way back to Castlerock they talked about the match and the dramatic finish. As Eoin stood at the door of the school waving to his father as he drove away, another car pulled up and Duffy and Flanagan jumped out.

'No red shirts in this school,' sneered Duffy.

'Even winning ones?' asked Eoin.

Duffy stopped and looked at Flanagan. He opened his mouth, but no words came.

'See you in the morning,' smiled Eoin, before he took the stairs two at a time on the way to bed.

CHAPTER 16

It was raining next morning, and a cold wind whipped in off Dublin Bay. Eoin shivered as he pulled on the green and white shirt of Castlerock College.

'Right team, gather around,' said Mr Carey as the clatter of studs echoed around the changing room.

'Ligouri College aren't the biggest school in this competition, but they have a decent record. We must not underestimate them. I want to see us getting on top from the off, and I want to see points on the board.

'Duffy, you better have your kicking boots on, and you need to take anything we get within range in the first twenty minutes.'

'Madden, you've had a good season so far, so let's see a bit more of that form at this level. Keep close to Duffy and be ready to get the moves going.'

As Mr Carey moved on to gee-up the forwards, Duffy stepped back and turned his head towards Eoin.

'The only time you'll see the ball today is at the kick off. Get used to it, loser,' he muttered under his breath.

Eoin jogged out on the field along with the rest of the team. There were a couple of hundred boys watching, including several members of the SCT.

Duffy kicked off and the ball fell short of the ten metre line, which meant the teams had to return to the middle for a scrum.

'Sloppy, Duffy,' roared Mr Carey, 'Sharpen up.'

Duffy winced, and some of the younger boys laughed at the bully's discomfort.

Ligouri turned out to be rather a good side, and actually took the lead with a penalty kick from almost halfway scored by an enormous No.8 with flaming red hair.

Duffy was kicking every time he got the ball, and missed touch on a couple of occasions. It became clear to Eoin that he was not going to pass to him. Inwardly he was rather glad about that, as no passes also meant there was no opportunity to drop the ball, or make a fool of himself once again.

'Get the line moving,' roared Mr Carey as the Castlerock out-half once again hoofed the ball up-field.

The next time the ball came back to Duffy, he tossed a pass way over Eoin's head to the outside centre, smirking as the ball fell into his hands and he sprinted away for a try.

'Good move, Duffy,' said Carey as he ran on with a water bottle while the kicker was preparing for the conversion. 'The missed pass caught them out. Keep playing like that and we'll win this.'

Duffy missed with the goal kick, and missed another penalty attempt shortly afterwards.

With the score 5–3 at half-time, Mr Carey was a little bit concerned.

'Duffy, what's wrong with your kicking today? If you're off-form with the boot there's no point kicking for touch every ball you get. The first time you let the backs run we got a try. I want to see a lot more of that in the second half.'

'Sir, to be honest I don't have confidence in my centre,' said Duffy, nodding towards Eoin. 'He's never played there before on this team and I don't think he's up to it.'

'All right Duffy, that's enough,' interrupted Mr Carey. 'I selected Madden because *I* think he's up to it. Now make sure he gets plenty of ball in the second half. Out you go.'

From the kick-off the Castlerock forwards won the chase for the ball and immediately formed a ruck. The ball came back to Vincent at scrum-half who tossed it out to Duffy.

The out-half made a break and dashed past two Ligouri tacklers. With Castlerock having three men outside shadowed by just two defenders, a try looked likely. Duffy threw the ball in the direction of Eoin, but about a foot higher than he expected it.

Eoin scrabbled at the ball as it bounced off his shoulder and forward onto the ground. The referee whistled for a knock-on, giving Ligouri College the scrum.

'Come on, Madden,' moaned Mr Carey, 'hang on to it.'

'Yeah,' smirked Duffy, 'hang on to it, you culchie slob.'

Eoin grimaced, and glared at Duffy. He knew the out-half had done that on purpose, but there was no point complaining.

The next time the ball came out, Eoin was ready for it and reacted quickly to gather it six inches off the ground, just below his knees. He steadied himself upright and threw an inch perfect pass out to the other centre, who crashed through a tackle to score a try.

'Excellent pass, Madden,' said Mr Carey as he trotted on once again.

The game ended 10-3 to Castlerock, but the coach was not overly delighted with the performance.

'We've a lot of work to do guys, and we especially

need to look at the way the backline moves. Extra practice for the backs tomorrow morning after mass.'

The team groaned, and changed in silence. Charlie looked over at Eoin and cast his eyes up to heaven with a grin. Lorcan caught the exchange and smiled too, Eoin was surprised, but pleased – maybe this team wasn't too bad after all.

As they left the changing room, Richie Duffy turned to face Eoin.

'You were lucky with that pass today, Madden, but no-one on this team wants you here. Don't make any long-term plans about that No.12 shirt.'

'If I were you,' replied Eoin, 'I'd be more worried about who's wearing the No.10 shirt on that performance.'

And with that, he turned and jogged out to where Alan and Rory were waiting, with a smile on his face wider than any of Duffy's failed kicks at goal.

CHAPTER 17

Training next morning was cancelled, to Eoin's relief, as the first snows of winter had started to roll in off Dublin Bay. It reminded Eoin that Christmas was just around the corner and he would soon be going home to Tipperary.

The next week was spent studying for tests, but Mr Carey told them at practice that the second round of the cup would be held on the Saturday after the end of term, so Eoin would have to delay his return home.

'Good news for you, Madden, we're playing away in Rostipp – not too far from your place I think?' Carey said.

Rostipp, thought Eoin, *that's where a few of the lads from primary school went. If they had taken up rugby, that would make it interesting.*

The Christmas exams went well enough for Eoin,

although he still struggled with Maths and was completely outfoxed by Mr Finn's History paper.

'I always mix up Daniel O'Connell and Charles
Stewart Parnell,' he explained to his father when he
called to the school to collect his cases on the last day
of term.

Mr Madden laughed and told his son not to worry.

'Mr Finn is a decent man, he knows how hard you've
been working.'

That shut Eoin up for a few seconds as they finished
packing the car.

'I hate having to stay over tonight,' he said, 'but Mr
Carey wants us all to go down on the bus together.'

'Don't worry,' said his dad, 'It's just one more night
and your mum and I will be there tomorrow.'

'And Grandad?' asked Eoin.

'Well ... I don't think he's up to it really. He's been
home a few weeks now, but he hasn't been out and a
trip like that might be too much for him. You'll see him
a lot when we get home – he's moved into your room!'

Eoin was a bit put out that he wouldn't be getting
his old room, but if there was anyone in the world he
would give it up for, it was his grandad.

He said goodbye to his dad, and wandered back into
the school. Most of his friends had left for home and just

Rory – who was on the bench for the As – remained in the Dixie Dorm.

'Well, Eoin,' he said, 'that was quite an introduction to Castlerock for you!'

'I know,' he replied, 'I think I would have preferred to keep my head down and stay on the Cs, but it's been fun some of the time.'

'Come on!' said Rory, 'There's hundreds of guys in this school who would love to have half your talent as a player. Forget the likes of Duffy and Flanagan, the rest of the school are delighted that you've come here, even if they don't know it yet.'

Eoin looked out the window as the last of the boarders drifted away. A knock came to the door.

'Madden, Grehan, come with me,' said Mr Carey, 'team meeting.'

They followed the coach downstairs to the dining hall, where the table was set for about thirty.

'The 13As are a fantastic group of players, in whom we have great hopes for the future,' said Mr McCaffrey. 'We've decided in the circumstances to throw a little Christmas party for a special group of young men.'

Eoin and Rory squeezed in at the end of the table just as a dozen of the teachers carried in plates piled high with turkey and ham.

'Do enjoy yourselves,' said Mr McCaffrey, 'But remember there's an important game at 1pm tomorrow in County Tipperary. We won't have any Christmas pudding or cake for you after this, and I hope you all get a good night's sleep and head into the holidays with another victory under your belts.'

An hour later Eoin and Rory hauled themselves upstairs with grave doubts about their ability to run anywhere fast within the next twenty-four hours.

'At least I'm just keeping the bench warm,' groaned Rory.

'At the rate David Vincent was tucking into seconds I'd say you've a good chance of starting,' came back Eoin.

Next morning Eoin was proved correct, as David Vincent was a peculiar shade of green when they all met up for breakfast. Richie Duffy waved a sausage in front of his face, which caused the scrum-half to leap from his seat and race out of the hall.

'Looks like you're the man today, Grehan,' sneered Duffy. 'You better be quick getting the ball out to me.' Rory turned an even darker shade of green than Vincent as Duffy's words sank in.

The bus journey down was quiet, with few takers for the sing-song Charlie Johnston tried to start several times.

Rory and Eoin sat at the back of the bus and, for once, it was Eoin doing all the reassuring. 'You'll be fine, Rory,' he said, 'You've had a great season on the Bs and our pack will mill these guys. Just keep it simple and give Duffy the ball – let *him* mess it up.'

'Yeah, but if he messes it up he'll blame me,' he groaned.

Eoin didn't have an answer to that.

The bus pulled into the school in Rostipp just as Eoin's mum and dad were parking their car. He queued to get off the bus, then he trotted over to them.

'Hi, Mum,' he called, backing away as his mother tried to give him a hug.

'Not in front of the guys, eh?' she chuckled, but with a little disappointment in her voice.

'I'd be dead if they saw that,' he replied.

'Good luck today, son,' said his dad, 'we'll be supporting you all the way. It'll be the first time I've ever watched a Madden play rugby.'

Eoin jogged away, realising that his father had never seen Dixie in action and couldn't tell him about all the great man's deeds like Mr Finn had.

The team changed into their green and white hoops and ran out to prepare for battle.

'Madden,' roared a voice from the other half of the

field, 'You're only a fairy.'

Eoin looked across to see a huge, red-faced boy in the colours of Rostipp. 'Curry' Ryan was famous in Ormondstown for his enormous appetite and the loudest laugh in the county.

'And you're only an oversized leprechaun,' he called back at him.

Duffy turned and glowered at Eoin.

'Shut up you culchie idiot,' he snarled. 'We don't want to banter with these yokels, we want their blood.'

Eoin turned his back on Richie Duffy and prepared for kick-off.

Rory looked even more nervous now he had seen that the Castlerock pack wouldn't have it their own way – even Eoin gulped as he saw how big the Tipperary twelve-year-olds were. 'Curry' Ryan was enormous, but even he had to tilt his head back to look at the pair of brothers who were playing in the second row.

Eoin's former primary school classmates, Roger and George Savage, were the youngest sons of a man who once played in goal for the Tipperary hurlers. Neither he nor his sons were the sharpest pencils in the pencil case, but he famously went two whole seasons without conceding a goal for the county. It looked like nothing much got past the sons either.

The game started cautiously, with Castlerock taking their time to assess their opponents. Rory was careful to ensure the ball went straight to Duffy's hands, and the out-half kicked the first three balls he received.

'OK, Duffy, time to bring the backs into it,' called out Mr Carey.

It became clear as the game went on that Rostipp were a limited side, and that there was little pace in their backline. The forwards were strong and pushed the Castlerock pack around, but Glen Fox at hooker was very quick with the heel and Rory was getting plenty of possession.

With ten minutes to the break Castlerock won a scrum and Rory flicked the ball quickly to Duffy, who was so surprised at how fast the ball came back that he instantly passed it on. Eoin realised that he had the ball in his hands for the first time in the game, and wasn't going to waste a rare opportunity.

The Rostipp centres looked nervously at each other as Eoin headed for the gap between them. He waited till the last moment when the two defenders dived, and his sidestep left the Rostipp players with only each other for company.

Eoin was through then, and jogged over the line to touch down under the posts. Duffy converted and at half-time the Dublin school were still 7-0 up.

'I'm not too happy with this,' griped Mr Carey, 'We're letting a far inferior team push us around and we're not playing to our strengths at all. You're getting great service from Grehan, Duffy, and you're not getting the ball out to the wings. This can't go on.'

Duffy started to speak, but closed his mouth and glowered back at the coach.

Castlerock started the second-half brightly and panicked Rostipp players gave away a string of penalties. The score stood at 16-3 to the visitors with five minutes remaining when Duffy made a huge mistake.

The Rostipp boys were forming a line-out when Duffy called out to Charlie Johnston, 'Get someone to sort out Rodge there – or is it Podge?'

The Savage brothers stopped and stared at Duffy. They took a couple of steps towards him before the referee whistled and ordered them back to their positions. The atmosphere on the field changed immediately, with real tension on the Rostipp side that their team-mates would do something appalling, and real fear among the Castlerock boys that they would suffer for their captain's stupidity.

The ball was deflected back to Rory from the line-out, and when he found Duffy the out-half couldn't get rid of the ball quick enough. His rapid delivery opened up more space for Eoin and after a couple of passes the ball found its way back to him. He saw a gap on the outside and went for it, sprinting along the touchline towards the try-line. Just as he got there he felt as if the sun had gone behind a cloud, as a huge figure loomed into view. Eoin dived towards the patch of grass in the corner and shouted 'yes' as the ball touched the turf.

His next roar came with extreme pain as he felt the green grass of Tipperary banging against his right side and a large rugby player crushing him into it from the left. Roger Savage stood up and looked down at Eoin.

'Sorry, Madden, I thought you were that out-half.'

Eoin couldn't speak, as his whole left hand side was in agony.

To his embarrassment, the first person who knelt down beside him was his mother, who had charged across the field when she heard his scream.

'Oh, my poor boy, are you all right?' she cried.

'It's sore,' said Eoin, 'But I think I'm all right.'

He stood up, but every time he moved, or even took a breath, a sharp pain shot through his side.

'It could be a rib,' said Mr Carey, 'We'll need to have him X-rayed.'

That was the end of Eoin's game and, once he had been examined in the local hospital, it looked like an enforced break in his new rugby career too. Roger Savage's bulk had cracked two of Eoin's ribs and he would need plenty of rest.

'There's nothing much we can do,' explained the doctor. 'The cracks have settled back already and we'll let biology take its course.'

Eoin was disappointed that there was none of the glamour of a plaster cast for his friends to sign, instead he had weeks away from anything energetic and pain every time he moved.

'Mr Carey rang,' his dad told him as they drove home that evening. 'He was just checking that you were all right. He seemed very disappointed that you'd be out for a few weeks. Oh yeah, and they won twenty-one three. He says they're playing Cedric's in the semi-final.'

When his dad said 'they're', Eoin realised that he had no chance of being in the team for the game. He would just have to hope he could get back on the team as soon as possible and force his way back in for the final.

He stepped gingerly from the car, every step a serious discomfort.

'I hear you've been in the wars,' came a voice from the sitting room as he walked through the front door.

'Grandad!' called out Eoin. 'Yes, I was knocked down by an oversized Rostipp bullock.'

'Tell me all about it,' said the old man, who was sitting in the armchair beside the fire wrapped in a blanket.

Eoin told the story of the game up to the injury, when his mother and father disappeared to the kitchen and garden.

'I had a cracked rib once,' his Grandad said. 'It was half-time in the Junior Cup final. The headmaster wouldn't let me go off, and they strapped it up in a half-mile of bandage. He gave me two aspirin and sent me back out!'

'And you won, of course,' said Eoin.

'Yes, that was a funny game. Not that I was laughing much at the end. The lads wanted to carry me off on their shoulders, but I had to run away because the rib hurt so much.'

Eoin winced as his ribs gave a twinge.

'Don't worry, lad,' said Dixie. 'They wouldn't be let do that sort of thing these days. You'll come back when you're ready.'

'The semi is in five weeks and the doctor told me to rest for six. I hope I've enough time to get back for the final at the end of February.'

'I'm sure you will, Eoin,' he replied. 'You're a big, strong lad and three weeks of your mother's home cooking will cure anything. Sure look at me, I'm thriving on it!'

CHAPTER 18

The Christmas holidays passed quickly, and Eoin had plenty of chats with his grandad about rugby. He had already heard lots of the stories from Mr Finn and the other teachers, but it was still fascinating to hear them from the mouth of the great Dixie.

Once, Eoin tried to ask why he had given up the game so suddenly, but his grandad just pursed his lips and shook his head.

'I'm sorry, Eoin,' he said, sadly. 'I promise I'll tell you, but I find it all very upsetting and I'm not in the whole of my health. Get yourself fit for that cup final and sure we'll have plenty of chances to chat before then.'

Eoin kept away from the subject then, deciding it was best to let his grandad tell him in his own time.

His ribs had stopped hurting every time he moved, although he still couldn't lift anything heavy or break into anything faster than a gentle trot. His dad carried his cases to the car on the day before term began.

'Good luck, Eoin,' called out his grandad, 'I'll be watching out for your scores.'

Eoin grinned and tapped his ribs. 'Give me a chance to get them right first. But it won't be long now – you were dead right about mum's cooking!'

The journey dragged, with traffic hold-ups all the way as the capital prepared to welcome back all those who had left for the holidays. It was dark by the time they reached Castlerock and Eoin was tired.

Mr Finn helped them lift the cases into the hall and took Mr Madden aside as Eoin went to find his pals.

'How's Dixie, Kevin?' he asked. 'I sent him a Christmas card, but I haven't heard anything back. Is he OK?'

'He's fine, Mr Finn,' Mr Madden replied. 'It's just that, back then, he cut everyone off, and has never talked it out. I see a great change in him though since Eoin started at Castlerock and he's really taken to watching the rugby again. He's in good form, but still very reluctant to visit the dark parts of his past. We'll just have to give him time.'

'Ah time, the great healer,' said Mr Finn.

'Yes, and I'm sure he'd be delighted to see you. We're planning a trip up to one of the Six Nations games, if he's in his health. And sure, who knows, maybe Eoin's team could make the Under 13A final. He wouldn't miss that.'

Eoin had persuaded Kevin and Fiachra to lift his cases up to the Dixie Dorm, at the cost of a packet of liquorice laces.

The trio sat on their beds munching the sweets and swapping stories about the holidays when Alan and Rory strolled in.

'Hey, Eoin, how's the spare ribs?' chuckled Rory. 'Maybe a bit of barbecue sauce might make it better!'

Eoin tossed a shoe, which skimmed Rory's red curls just as he ducked.

'Hey careful now, we don't want to lose another star player off the 13As, do we?' said Rory; he grinned as Alan explained that Mr Carey had just pinned up the 13A panel for second-term and Rory was down as first-choice scrum-half.

'I bet David Vincent is feeling sicker now,' laughed Eoin.

Eoin wandered down to watch the first training session the next day, and the pain in his ribs got worse as he watched.

Mr Carey came over to ask him about his progress as Flanagan dropped the ball for the third time in ten minutes.

'Hurry back, Eoin, we need you pretty badly,' he said, casting his eyes upwards.

'I will sir, it shouldn't be long now,' grinned Eoin.

But Eoin's recovery was not as quick as he had hoped. Miss O'Dea took him down to the local hospital for an X-Ray which showed that one of the cracked ribs still hadn't knitted.

'Another two weeks, I'd say,' explained the doctor, 'and no rugby for two weeks after that.'

'But that means I'll definitely miss the semi and have less than a week before the final,' Eoin moaned.

'I'm sorry, Eoin, but ribs can be tricky,' the doctor explained. 'A cracked rib is a weakened bone, and if you were to break it, you could cause serious internal injuries. You'll have plenty more chances to play rugby.'

Eoin was devastated, and Mr Carey even more so when he told him that evening.

'Ah, that's terrible news, Eoin. You've made such fantastic progress this year and you bring real flair and imagination to that backline. I hope they can squeak past St Cedric's in the semi and sure maybe you'll be right for Lansdowne Road ...'

It was only at that moment that Eoin realised that the final would be held at the Aviva Stadium.

'Wow, I never knew that the final would be there!' he said.

'Yes, it's being played this year as the warm-up game for the crowd before Leinster's Heineken Cup game against Lourdes,' explained Mr Carey.

'Well, I hope I don't need a miracle to be ready for it,' said Eoin, smiling as Mr Carey went back to the training.

The semi-final against St Cedric's was held in Castlerock, and there were hundreds of boys and their parents gathered around the pitch. Eoin was allowed to join the replacements on the bench, and he noticed his ribs no longer stung when he sat down.

Rory had indeed held his place on the team, but he was no longer quite as friendly to Alan and Eoin in class or in the Dixie Dorm. In the dressing-room before the game, Eoin realised why.

Rory was sitting in the corner beside Richie Duffy, and the two were whispering to each other and laughing as they dressed for battle.

Eoin walked over to his friend, and wished him luck.

Rory looked up from tying his bootlaces, saw it was Eoin, and shrugged. 'Whatever,' he muttered.

'How's the soft boy with the broken ribs?' sneered Duffy. 'Better luck next year.'

Rory laughed.

Eoin turned away, annoyed that Rory could be so cruel, and so stupid.

Out on the field the half-back pairing were just as close, and the combination seemed to be working well. Duffy continued to kick too often, and Mr Carey continued to shout at him for doing so.

St Cedric's was a small school, but always produced strong teams and this year was no different. The score was level at half-time, 10–10, and remained so until eight minutes before the end.

Castlerock won a scrum close to the opposition line, and Charlie Johnston kept the ball at his feet as the pack drove forward. About four feet from the try-line, Rory snatched the ball from between Charlie's ankles, twisted and dived low through the Cedric's scrum-half's legs. The ball was grounded on the line and Castlerock were ahead.

Duffy converted and time ran out before St Cedric's could score again. As the final whistle blew the Castlerock boys pounced on Rory and lifted them over their heads. The tiny, red-head screamed with delight and was still laughing throughout the lap of honour as the school hailed a new hero.

When they finally set him down, Eoin was there to

stick a hand out in congratulation. Rory looked from side to side, saw Duffy staring at him, and turned his back on Eoin.

'Fair enough, Rory, have it that way if you like,' Eoin muttered. 'But don't coming running to me when you're out of favour again.'

CHAPTER 19

Rory's decision to join the Duffy gang made life quite awkward in the Dixie Dorm. There were four weeks to the final, and Mr Carey had the 13As out for training every evening after school. He asked Eoin along to be part of the tactical discussions, but it was hard to concentrate after a day in class, and when your best friend on the team has jumped ship.

'How is the injury?' Mr Carey asked as they walked back to the school after one training session.

'Much better sir, there's no pain even when I laugh,' Eoin replied.

'There's no danger of you laughing at these sessions, is there? I've never seen you looking so miserable. Is everything all right?'

'Yes, sir, everything's fine,' he lied.

Back in the dorm, Rory tried to be friendly, but Eoin and Alan had enough of his double playing.

'Look, Rory, cutting me dead 'cos Duffy is watching is so stupid,' said Eoin, 'We're not in senior infants here.'

'You know what sort of pup Duffy is, and you've chosen to become just like him,' said Alan. 'Fire away, but don't expect us to be your buddy when you get back to the Dixie Dorm.'

Rory looked at Anton and Fiachra for support, but they were just as grim-faced as the others.

Rory grunted, shrugged his shoulders, and lay down on his bed and stuck in his iPod earphones.

Ten days before the big game, Eoin was summoned to see Miss O'Dea at the staffroom.

'Mr Carey has asked me to organise an X-Ray for you today,' she said. 'I'll take you down to the hospital, but I'm afraid I can't stay – will you be OK to get the Dart back to the school?'

'I'm sure I will,' Eoin replied. 'When do we leave?'

'Right now,' she said, 'do you mind missing double Maths?'

Eoin grinned and followed the teacher outside towards her small red Mini.

Miss O'Dea showed him into the ultrasound department and, as soon as he was signed in, she checked that he knew the way to the Dart station and back to the school.

The morning dragged as Eoin spent most of his time staring at posters about healthy eating and activities. He should have brought a book, he realised, even a Maths book.

The X-Ray took a few minutes and then he was back to the corridor to wait. After an hour a tall doctor came out and introduced himself as Dr Shukla.

'OK, Eoin, it looks like you are completely healed,' he said, holding two sets of X-Rays against a lightbox on the wall. 'Any pain?'

'No, doctor,' he said. 'Would it be OK If I went back to rugby?'

The doctor frowned. 'Well .. that mightn't be such a good idea. Have you been exercising much?'

'Well, no .... said Eoin.

'Hmmm ... You see your muscles won't be back to their best, and you just won't be as fit after seven or eight weeks off activity. I'd say get back to some light jogging for a week or two before you start back training. What's the rush?'

Eoin told him about the final in Lansdowne Road just ten days away.

Dr Shukla's face fell. 'Oh, that's very, very soon for an injury such as this. I think it would be a mistake to try to get back so quickly.'

Eoin shrugged his shoulders and let out a big sigh, 'OK, Dr Shukla, thank you very much anyway.'

'There's always the cricket season!' the doctor joked.

'Not in Ormondstown there isn't,' Eoin fired back.

Eoin crossed the dual carriageway and walked through the leafy lanes to the train station. He was still in torment over missing the big game, as he really wanted his grandad to come up to watch him play.

He took the next train and was staring glumly out the window when he noticed they had arrived in a station named 'Lansdowne Road'.

'Oh no,' he realised. 'This is heading north – into the city!'

He dashed off the train in time to see a southbound train pull out of the station. He checked the timetable – the next one wasn't for almost an hour. Already frustrated by his hospital stay, Eoin decided he would kill the time, and begin his road back to fitness, by taking a jog out the gates of the station.

As he trotted onto the road outside, he spied a gate open in the stadium walls, and his natural curiosity took him through it. He emerged behind the West Stand, and while there were a few people milling around they were all too busy to notice him.

'I wonder is Brian about?' Eoin thought aloud, as he wandered through the tunnel towards the arena.

'Yes, I am,' came a voice as Brian appeared from behind a pillar.

'Wow, that was pretty neat,' said Eoin, 'I never heard you coming.'

'What has you here on a midweek morning,' asked Brian, 'have they thrown you out of that school?'

'I wish!' said Eoin. 'No, I got the wrong train and got off at this station to go back. But there's no Dart for ages. I thought I'd come in to see what was going on.'

'It's quiet today,' said Brian, 'but there's a couple of big games coming up.'

'Sure, don't I know,' interrupted Eoin, 'I might be playing in one myself on the day of the Leinster game. The 13A final.'

'Gosh,' said Brian, 'That's wonderful. Why the "might" though?'

'I've just come from the hospital. I'm only back after cracking a couple of ribs against Rostipp,' explained.

'That shower of bowsies, always a tough bunch the Rostippers,' grinned Brian. 'Did you ever try comfrey? That was a herb we used to use to treat cuts and breaks. Fierce powerful stuff. Mash it up with water in a poultice. Give it a go.'

The pair wandered out through the darkened players' tunnel into the bright, sunlit stadium. They sat down in the grandstand; Eoin in the row in front of Brian. He noticed how pale Brian's legs were, and how ridiculously old-fashioned his boots.

'Were did you get those things?' Eoin asked, pointing at the antique footwear.

'I got them in Elvery's in Nassau Street,' Brian replied, 'Thirty bob they cost me.'

'What's a *bob*?' asked Eoin, puzzled.

'It's a shilling,' said Brian. 'Of course, it's all euros nowadays I believe.'

'When exactly did you buy those boots?' asked Eoin, starting to get a little anxious, but not knowing quite why.

'I bought them in the sales – New Year's Day 1928 I believe. My brothers gave me a pound each for Christmas ...'

'1928?' quizzed Eoin, 'What do you mean?'

'It was a few months before the accident ... Yes, March 1928 that was,' Brian confirmed.

Eoin was rooted in his seat.

'B-b-but that was more than eighty years ago ... how old *are* you?' he said, quietly.

'I'm twenty-two, of course,' said Brian, 'the same age as I was when I died.'

CHAPTER 20

Eoin's eyes widened. 'You're *dead*? Are you a ghost?'

'I suppose I am,' said Brian, 'But I never really thought about it. I've just hung around here since it happened ...'

'Since *what* happened,' asked Eoin, whose knuckles had turned white as he clung to the plastic seat.

'I should have told you before this,' Brian nodded. 'But I didn't want to frighten you off. Let's go up the back of the stand here, there's a great view of the whole stadium.'

Eoin's mind was a whirl; on one hand he wanted to run away screaming, but his in-built curiosity was kicking in.

Brian sat down at the very back of the stand, and pointed to the near touchline.

'It was just about there,' he said, 'about five yards in. 'I came here after I left school, my old school pal Ned brought me along. We had great sport on the second team, and won the Metro the year before. But Lansdowne had a fantastic team, and the best set of backs of any club in the world. We had Ernie Crawford, Jack Arigho ... legends,' he said. 'We were playing Trinity. It was a big game, my first cup match for the first team.'

Eoin had many questions, but didn't say a word.

'It was a cold day, and the ground was hard. We gave as good as we got for the first ten minutes or so. And then ...'

Brian looked Eoin in the eye, then dropped his head.

'And then there was a scrum. Now in those days the scrum was a rough-house. It was a tough place, and you had to show you were top dog. There was none of this "touch, pause, engage" lark. The packs would just run at each other, charging like a pair of goats butting heads.'

Eoin stared, finding it hard to imagine the scene.

'Well, the trouble with that was that you had to collide precisely, so your heads would interlock and the scrum could form. That day we didn't meet quite right, and somebody slipped and the scrum collapsed. Whatever way it fell I was caught ...'

'And it killed you?' asked Eoin, gently.

'No, not quite,' explained Brian. 'When they all stood up I was still on the ground and couldn't move. I told the referee, Mr Bell, that I had no power in my body. They got the stretchers on and I was carried over to the touchline. There was a lot of fuss and then a motor ambulance arrived and took me to hospital. I saw a doctor who told me I was very badly hurt, and that the nurses would make me comfortable. To be honest, I wasn't in any pain, and the shock of it all meant I didn't really take it in. My mother and father were already deceased, and all I had in the world were my two brothers, Charlie and Edgar. Charlie was on the Irish team at that stage, he was a great player. I asked the nurses could they contact the lads, and they said they were already on the way. The two lived down in Athlone and Cork, but I really wanted to see them and was glad to hear they were coming.

'A few of the team came in to see me after the game, and I was delighted to hear we had won 13-0. We chatted about the scrum, but I insisted that nobody was to blame and that it was just one of those things.

'Eddie and Charlie arrived during the evening, but I was very tired by then and I didn't really want to talk. They sat by the bed all night, but by morning time I wasn't able to open my eyes anymore and I slipped away.

'It's a strange thing, dying. One minute I was lying in bed, and then I was floating above looking down at everyone. The lads were very sad – I was their baby brother – but I didn't really understand what was going on.'

Eoin stared at his feet, not knowing what to say.

'I was upset after a while, when I realised that I wouldn't play rugby again, or go to the silent pictures with my pals. I watched the funeral, and hung around afterwards in the graveyard. But the next morning I woke up here in the Lansdowne dressing room, and I've been here ever since.'

'And what have you been doing for the past eighty years?' asked Eoin.

'Well, I've had a front-row seat for every single match that has been played here since my last game. I even jumped over onto the touchline for a few of the more exciting ones. I saw some fantastic players here over the years, you know.'

'And did you ever talk to anyone?' the boy asked.

'Well, that's the queerest thing,' Brian replied, 'Nobody ever saw me until you walked into the first aid room a few months back. That gave me quite a shock. I've really enjoyed our chats, and they've given me a new lease of, eh, life,' he grinned. 'I'll give you a hand if you're playing in that final too,' he said. 'Maybe I could trip up the opposition, or lob another ball into the scrum to confuse them!'

'That might just confuse our lads too,' Eoin laughed.

The schoolboy paused, not sure what to say next.

'Eh, Brian,' he hesitated, 'Did you ever see a player called Dixie Madden play for Castlerock?'

Brian's grey eyes widened. 'I did, and a brilliant player he was too. Why do you ask?'

'He's my grandad,' Eoin explained.

'Ah, of course, he was a Tipperary man, I should have guessed. I saw him play many big schools' games here, and I never saw a better out-half for his age. He was brilliant. And then one day I came out to watch the Old Castlerock team and he wasn't there, and I never saw him again. I often wonder what happened to him ....'

'Me too,' said Eoin, 'And I'm going to find out.'

CHAPTER 21

Eoin was still in a blur when he found his way back to the school, just in time to hear the bell for end of classes.

'What kept you?' quizzed Alan. 'That was some long X-Ray.'

'Don't talk,' said Eoin. 'I was hours in that hospital. Bored stupid I was.'

'Stupid is the word,' sneered Richie Duffy, as he barged past the pair of friends. 'The man who missed the cup final because of a cracked rib. *Lo-ser.*'

Eoin held himself back, but couldn't control his tongue.

'You know you've no chance without me, Duffy. Your sister could cut open the St Osgur's defence better than you can. You better say your prayers that I'm ready.'

Duffy stared at him, but his own tongue wasn't as quick as Eoin's and he opened and closed his mouth like a goldfish.

At that moment Mr Finn arrived, and gave Eoin a quizzical look.

'Is everything all right, gentlemen?' he snapped.

'Yes, sir,' Eoin and Richie chorused.

'Move along then, Mr Duffy, you must have training to go to,' he said, directing him towards the playing fields.

When Duffy had left, Mr Finn turned to Eoin. 'Be careful with that boy, Eoin, he is prone to hiding his inarticulacy behind his fists.'

'Thank you, sir. I understand,' Eoin replied.

'How is Dixie? I wrote to him, but haven't received a reply.'

'He's a bit better I think. He said he'd come up for the final if I was on the team....'

'And what are the chances of that?'

'Well, according to the doctor I shouldn't be playing ...' he sighed.

And then he thought of something.

'What's comfrey, sir, and where could I get some?'

'Gosh that's a word I haven't heard in years,' said Mr Finn, 'Where on earth did you hear about that?'

'A ... eh ... an ... *old man* told me it would help to heal my ribs,' he replied.

'Well, yes, we used it all the time on injuries when I was young,' the teacher said. 'It grew in ditches and along the canal banks. There may even be some down by the stream at the back of the school ... I tell you what, I'll take a walk down there this evening and if I find any I'll let you know. Sure it's worth trying – it sounds like it could be your only chance.'

'Thank you, Mr Finn,' Eoin replied, suddenly cheered up.

Hours later, Eoin was lying on his bed trying to read a comic book, but his mind kept returning to Brian and his extraordinary, if sad, story. He had always believed in ghosts, and Grandad Madden was full of great stories about the fairies, banshees and pookas that lived in the woods they passed on their walks. But it was still a bit weird to meet and talk to one, especially one as friendly as Brian.

A knock came to the door.

'Come in,' Alan shouted, and then apologised for being so loud when Mr Finn walked in.

'Eoin, come with me,' he said.

Eoin jumped up from his bed, puzzled at the teacher's strange manner.

Outside the door, Mr Finn carefully closed the door behind him.

'I'm sorry, Eoin, I've just had a call from your father. Dixie has taken a turn and won't be able to make the match next week.

'In fact, he is quite ill. Your dad asked me could he come tomorrow to take you home, but I refused to let him drive all the way up. I'll drive you down in the morning. I would so like to see Dixie again.'

Eoin gulped and fought back tears. 'Thank you, sir, I'll see you after breakfast.'

He tried hard to sleep that night, but found it impossible. Every time he closed his eyes he saw his grandad lying in the hospital bed. He tossed over in his mind the recent conversations and how much he wanted to talk rugby with the great Dixie Madden.

Next morning, Mr Finn was waiting at the bottom of the staircase.

'I thought we'd make an early start, Eoin. We can get breakfast on the way.'

Eoin was relieved that he didn't have to face the rest of the school, particularly with Duffy gunning for him.

On the way they talked of rugby, and history, and living in Dublin. Mr Finn steered clear of school affairs, and of Grandad Madden's mysterious past. He was a careful driver, and with the stop for breakfast it took almost three hours to reach Ormondstown.

Dixie was being cared for in the small local hospital, and Eoin directed Mr Finn through its gates in time to see his father coming out the main door.

'He's sleeping now, thank God,' Mr Madden said, 'He's had a bad night though. Kept asking when you'd be down.'

He turned to the teacher.

'Thank you very much, Mr Finn, for bringing Eoin down. I told dad that you were driving down this morning and he said he'd like to see you too. It really perked him up. Come on back to the house and have a cup of tea. We can come here again in an hour.'

The trio drove back to the Maddens' house, where Eoin's mother embraced her son at the door.

'You poor lad ...' she said, before remembering his injured ribcage and jumping backwards, '... oh, I hope I haven't made them any worse!'

Eoin grinned. 'No, Mam, I'm almost right. I was at the hospital yesterday and the doctor told me to wait another two to four weeks. The final is in nine days so I'm hoping for a miracle ...'

'Oh, silly me, I almost forgot,' said Mr Finn, taking a plastic bag from his pocket. 'I found a whole clump of comfrey down by the stream last night. It's not in flower yet, but the leaves are what do you good.'

'My mother used to swear by comfrey, "knitbone" she used to call it,' Mrs Madden said, 'I think you chop it up and make a poultice, don't you?'

While Mr Finn was overseeing the herbal recipe in the kitchen, Mr Madden took his son outside.

'Dixie has been talking of nothing else but this match for weeks now. I couldn't bear to tell him that your injury might keep you out. He told me he wants to tell you the whole story too. Last night, when he was bad, he told me that I was to explain it all to you if he didn't make it. God willing he'll have his health soon and be able to tell you the whole story. But don't push him in the hospital, he's very weak.'

'Ah Dad, I wouldn't do that,' said Eoin, 'if he wants to tell me he'll do it in his own good time. I always knew that.'

Inside, Mrs Madden pointed to a blob of green mush sitting on a saucer when Eoin and his father returned.

'There you are, Eoin, that's your lunch.'

Eoin's face turned just as green, but when he saw Mr Finn and his parents breaking into a grin he realised he had been fooled.

'No, you loo-lah,' his mother said, 'It's a poultice; I'll wrap it in a piece of linen and strap it to your ribs.'

'Won't it ooze out onto my shirt,' Eoin complained as

his mother rigged up the herbal remedy.

'You'll be fine,' his mother explained, 'and even if you do can't you just say you're a true Irishman with green blood.'

CHAPTER 22

The Maddens, with Mr Finn following behind, pulled into the car park of Ormondstown General Hospital shortly before 1pm. The sun had just emerged from behind a grey cloud and Eoin forced a smile onto his face, realising it was important not to look upset or worried in front of his grandad.

The old man was surrounded by pipes and wires when Eoin and his dad entered the ward. Dixie seemed to be asleep, but perhaps sensing the arrival of his only son – and only grandson – he slowly opened his eyes.

'Ah Eoin, how wonderful it is that you could come. And Andy Finn drove you all the way? What a great chum he is.'

'Mr Finn is outside, Dad,' Kevin told him, 'He wanted to let me in first. He's dying to see you too.'

'Dying to see me? I hope not,' the old man chuckled. 'There's enough of us dying around here.'

'Now, Dad, enough of that talk,' Kevin said. 'The doctor says you're good for another twenty years – four Rugby World Cups anyway. You might even get another Grand Slam out of it.'

'Grand Slam?' the old man snorted, 'Get out of that. Not a chance. *You'll* be lucky to see another one of them,' he directed at Eoin.

'Great to see you back to normal, Grandad!' laughed Eoin, 'There's nothing wrong with your spirit anyway!'

'Indeed, young man. That sleep gave me a great boost. Sit down there beside the bed and we'll have that chat.'

'Hang on, Dad, are you sure you're strong enough?' interrupted Kevin.

'I am, so go off and get yourself and Andy a cup of tea, and leave me with the boy. I have a lot to get through with this young man.'

Dixie and Eoin Madden looked into each other's eyes. The old man saw a bright, independent spirit, eager to learn. The boy saw a sadness, but behind it lay a light that was fighting hard to stay lit, because it realised it had so much shining still to do.

'I hated rugby,' Dixie said, 'hated it with a vicious, powerful, hurtful hatred. And it was stupid, I now know, because it wasn't rugby that took her away ....'

Eoin sat silently by the bed. His eye kept being dragged

away by the digital readouts on the machines monitoring Dixie's health.

'It was the winter of nineteen sixty-eight, sixty-nine. We were living in Dublin at the time, I was working for the bank in Rathmines and playing my rugby up with Old Castlerock. Kevin – your dad – had been born the summer before, but there were ferocious snows all winter long and we hardly got a chance to take him out for fresh air. The rugby was going well, very well really ... and I was lucky enough to be picked for the final Irish trial up in Lansdowne Road. The Saturday before was a rare sunny day and we had a game at home against the university. It really was a lovely day ....'

The old man paused, and rubbed his eyes.

'There were two Irish selectors there to watch, and the lads kept ribbing me that I would be getting a new green jersey, and Irene had better not wash it with the nappies. All harmless teasing, I suppose ... Anyway, the game was going well, and we were well on top. Just after the second half started a shocking wind got up, and started playing havoc with the kicking.

'I noticed at half-time that your grandmother, Irene, had arrived, and she gave me a little wave. Kevin was in the pram, an enormous black thing with a bouncy suspension. A lot of the other wives and girlfriends were around her, goo-gooing at the baby.

'I was concentrating on the game, up the other end of the pitch, when I heard this unmerciful crack. It was like a bomb going off. The game stopped, everyone turned and saw that a huge branch had broken off near the top of an old willow tree that stood beside the rugby pitch.

'It teetered for a couple of seconds, before down it tumbled. It was just as it started to fall that I saw that it was Irene who was standing underneath the tree, talking to another woman. As the branch crashed down through the tall tree I saw that she realised the danger and pushed the pram away. She only had a second or two, but she clearly decided that she had to save little Kevin ...'

Dixie paused, looking out the window for a moment, before resuming his story.

'And then the branch fell down, right on top of her.'

'I sprinted those sixty yards faster than anyone ever has, but there wasn't even a breath left in her when I got there. She had been killed stone dead.

'Somebody called an ambulance, but she was already gone. I held her in my arms for a few minutes, but then I heard Kevin crying and knew I had to go to him. It was a terrible day, terrible ...'

Eoin reached across and put his hand across the back

of Dixie's. He felt awful that the old man had dragged up such painful memories for him. And that he had never really thought about why he only had one grand-mother.

His grandfather looked him in the eyes again.

'And that was the last time I ever wore rugby kit, or even kicked a ball,' he said. 'I blamed myself at first, because Irene would never have been near that field that day had I not been playing. People talked me out of that notion, but I just hated the idea that she had lost her life, and we had lost all our dreams of a life together, over something as stupid as a game of rugby football.'

Dixie sighed and stared out the window.

'I even got visitors from the IRFU trying to talk me out of it. They thought I was a future Irish captain, they told me.

'I burnt all my rugby kit, my boots, even my school team photographs – which I regret most of all. And I wouldn't let Kevin play the game, imagine that?' he asked.

'Well, I don't think he would have been any good at it,' Eoin smiled.

'True,' agreed Dixie, 'but it was selfish of me to deny him the opportunity of playing a game that had given me such a lot. And taken away a lot from me, too, I suppose.'

'I don't think Dad minds,' said Eoin. 'He's becoming a keen supporter, but I don't think he has any regrets that he never played.'

'That's why I was so keen that you go to Castlerock too,' Dixie explained. 'I knew you would take to rugby, and I confess that I've been watching a lot of the sport again this winter, trying to catch up with the changes. It is a very different game to the one I said goodbye to back in 1969.

'I really hope I can get back to full health by the end of next week,' Dixie grinned. 'I wouldn't want to miss the chance of seeing the first Madden at Lansdowne Road in more than forty years.'

Eoin's face fell for a second, but he quickly composed himself, 'I'd love that, Grandad; I really hope you can make it.'

They talked for a while longer about sport and school, before Eoin heard a cough behind him, and his father appeared in the doorway.

'Hello, Dad, I hope Eoin's not tiring you too much?' Kevin asked. 'Andy Finn is here too and he'd love a quick word. He says he has to get back to Dublin before dark so he won't stay long.'

Eoin stood and watched as the two old pals, torn apart by tragedy and separated by half a lifetime of regret, renewed their friendship.

'God, Dixie, you're looking fantastic. I had heard you weren't well, but they were obviously mistaken …' joked Mr Finn.

Dixie laughed again, and the pair began to bridge the lost years.

Kevin gave the old men twenty minutes alone together before he called a halt, and hugs and handshakes ended the emotional afternoon.

'I hope this hasn't been too much for you today, Dad?' Kevin asked, after the teacher and pupil left.

'Not at all, not at all,' smiled his father. 'It has been an absolute tonic.'

And Dixie was right. The visit of Eoin and Andy had perked him up so much that the next time a nurse checked his vital signs it was apparent the old man was well on the road to recovery.

CHAPTER 23

As they started on their journey back to Dublin, Eoin and Mr Finn were in great form, as both had been enormously heartened by the visit to Dixie.

'What a fantastic man Dixie is,' Mr Finn kept saying. 'It is the main regret of my life that I didn't keep up our friendship. We never fell out, but he just removed himself totally from Castlerock. Then he left Dublin and we never met again. Even when your dad was at the school he never came to visit.'

Eoin felt freer now to talk about Dixie's career, and Mr Finn filled him in on many of the gaps. He confirmed that Dixie had been on the verge of a glorious career in a green shirt, and that the IRFU bigwigs had come to try to coax him back to the game. Eoin told the teacher about how Dixie had so regretted burning his photographs, and Mr Finn shook his head slowly.

'Grief is a terrible thing Eoin, I can't blame Dixie for

not wanting to see an oval ball again. Like everyone else I was very sorry that he never got a chance to play for Ireland, but my real regret in the end was for our friendship. That was far more important to me.

'I missed playing with him too, and to be honest rugby didn't have the same appeal for me for much longer either. I gave up at the end of the following season after we lost the senior cup final to Lansdowne.'

The mention of one of Dublin's oldest clubs reminded Eoin of something.

'Did you ever hear of a player called Hanrahan who played for Lansdowne?' he asked the teacher.

Mr Finn glanced across at Eoin, with a strange look on his face.

'I did indeed, how ever did you hear about him?'

Eoin thought quickly. 'I ... I was reading about him in the library,' he lied.

'And what did you read?' quizzed Mr Finn.

'That he was killed in Lansdowne Road,' Eoin replied.

'Yes, he was. Another very sad story. Brian Fitzgerald Hanrahan,' Mr Finn sighed. 'He was a Tipperary man, just like you. Long before my time, but people spoke very highly about him as a player. The strange thing is, the last time I heard his name spoken was just after your grandmother was killed.'

Eoin stared back at his teacher, unsure where this conversation might lead.

'It was about a week after the funeral, and I was around at Dixie's house. He was in an awful state, completely swamped by the grief of it all. A knock came to the door and I went to open it. There were two men at the door, wearing long dark coats.

'I invited them in and introduced them to Dixie. One of them was the IRFU president, but the other man, who was much older, did all the talking. He said his name was Charlie Hanrahan, and that he had seen Dixie in action on many occasions.

'He said he wanted to sympathise with Richard on his terrible loss, and to offer the union's support in any and every way. Dixie wasn't happy to see them at first, but I made them tea and they all came into the kitchen.

'Mr Hanrahan told Dixie that the whole rugby community joined him in mourning his loss, and would be standing with him for the rest of his days. He told him that he, too, had suffered a terrible tragedy through the game and that it was his fellow players who kept him going through the grief.

'He went on to tell us the story of his brother Brian, who died after suffering a terrible injury out on the field in Lansdowne Road. Charlie himself was in Limerick that day, playing for Dolphin, and didn't hear about the accident until he got home to Cork that night. A friend drove him up to Dublin where he arrived barely in time to say goodbye to his little brother.

'Charlie told us that he never wanted to play again, and pulled out of the Ireland team to play Wales the following weekend. Brian had been picked for Leinster to play Munster in a junior interpro on that very same day, would you believe. Charlie said he couldn't bear to even look at a ball for weeks afterwards.

'But his friendships in rugby kept him going, and he eventually took his place in the front row and played for Ireland twenty times over the next few seasons. "I don't doubt that I wouldn't be here at all if it wasn't for my pals," he told Dixie.'

'They didn't stay long, but strongly pressed Dixie on how glittering a future he had in rugby. They even suggested that he would captain Ireland one day ...'

'And that's why he never played again, is it?' asked Eoin.

'Well, I can't be sure, but that night Dixie cried harder than he ever cried before. I had to stay in the house with him I was so concerned about him. He just couldn't see any sort of future for himself without Irene, and playing rugby definitely wasn't going to help.

'I called over a couple of days later and found him out the back, burning his rugby gear in a big oil drum. He just looked at me and turned away.

'The next day I called he was gone. I heard after a while that he had asked the bank for a transfer and moved to County Tipperary. And that's the last time I saw him, until this afternoon. I'll never forget the look of pain in his eyes as he stoked that bonfire. He was lost, totally lost.'

Eoin remained silent for several minutes, and Mr Finn stared far ahead, trying to concentrate on the road ahead, but finding his mind racing back over the decades to the anguish of his dearest friend.

CHAPTER 24

That night, as he was going to bed, Eoin took care to undress in the bathroom. He didn't want Rory – or any of his room-mates, really – seeing the green slimy bandage that lay under his shirt. He took the poultice off carefully, and hid it in an empty crisp bag before dumping it in the waste basket. He rubbed his hand along his rib-cage. There was no longer even the slightest twinge.

As he lay in bed, he stared at the ceiling and went over the many new things he had learned that day. He felt an enormous sadness for his grandad – and his own dad – for their terrible loss. He felt slightly ashamed that he had never really noticed the absence of his second grandmother, and had never thought to ask why she wasn't there on Christmas morning or birthdays.

He thought about Brian too, and how his help had transformed him as a player. Wasn't it strange the way the Hanrahan story had weaved its way into his family history and had returned many years later? He desperately wanted to see Brian again.

The following morning he bumped into Mr Carey on his way to class.

'Madden, how are those ribs? What did the doc say?'

'Well, sir, he said I probably wouldn't be ready for the final, but that I could check it out next week,' he fibbed.

'Well get Miss O'Dea to book you an appointment for Tuesday morning. If you get the go-ahead it will give you three days to train.'

Eoin spent much of the weekend out jogging, stretching the muscles that had become lazy and underused during his long spell out of action. He ran down to the stream to stock up on the comfrey herb, making up his own mixture locked in the top-floor loo on a quiet Sunday morning.

As he applied the poultice, a knock came to the door. Almost spilling the green sludge, Eoin asked 'Who's that?'

'It's Alan,' came the reply, 'what on earth are you doing up here?'

'I could ask you the same thing – are you following me?' said Eoin, opening the door.

'Well, yes, I suppose I am,' Alan replied. 'I was a bit

worried about you. You were talking in your sleep last night ...'

Eoin went a deep shade of red. 'Really? Oh God, what was I saying?'

'I haven't a clue. You seemed to be talking about ghosts or something. It was very weird.'

Eoin went an even deeper shade, almost purple. 'That's mad; it must have been something I ate last night.'

'What exactly are you doing skulking around the top corridor?' Alan asked.

'Oh, well to tell you the truth I was just putting on this bandage,' showing Alan the green poultice. 'I didn't want Duffy's "eyes and ears" to know. It's an old wives' cure for cracked ribs or something. It seems to be working, too.'

'Brilliant — do you think there's still a chance you could make the team?' Alan asked.

'Yeah, I'm sure of it now. I've conned Carey into getting another X-Ray done on Tuesday and I'll be back in the running then ...'

On Monday evening, Alan and Eoin walked out of the dining hall after an unexciting dinner of chicken and pasta. A crowd was gathered around the noticeboard.

'Who is this A. N. Other guy?' a junior school pupil asked.

'Idiot! – Can't you read? It means "another". That means the place still hasn't been decided,' some one else replied.

Alan wormed his way to the front of the crowd.

'It's the team for the 13A final,' he called back to Eoin. 'And it looks like Mr Carey is going to wait for you.'

The team sheet carried fourteen names, but the strange name – traditionally used by uncertain selectors – was written beside No.12.

Eoin smiled, and headed off to change for another training run.

On Wednesday morning, he was again driven down to the hospital by Miss O'Dea, who gave him the fare for his Dart back to the school. Dr Shukla was very welcoming, and his face was puzzled when he returned with the X-Rays after a long delay.

'This is very strange, Eoin, I've had to go back to check the machine wasn't out of order,' he said.

'Is there something wrong,' Eoin said, looking worried.

'No, not at all. Your X-Rays are perfect. It is just that I would have expected there to be some sign of the previous injury, but this looks as if nothing at all has happened to your ribs since the day you were born. It is quite uncanny, unlike anything I've ever seen before ...'

Eoin smiled. 'Does that mean I'll be OK to play rugby next weekend?'

'You'll be OK to go out and play rugby *today* if you wish,' grinned Dr Shukla.

Eoin was bouncing as he arrived at the train station. He wanted to get back to school to tell Mr Carey as soon as possible. But just as he went to pay, he remembered Brian and how much he wanted to talk to him.

'Lansdowne Road,' he spluttered to the ticket attendant.

The train pulled up in the shadow of the stadium a few minutes later, and Eoin made his usual unannounced entry to the arena. He wandered around the tunnels and walked to the top of the stand, but Brian was nowhere to be seen. He even braved a trip to the VIP lounge and the First Aid room, but still the long-dead rugby player's spirit failed to make an appearance.

Eoin had been more than an hour at the stadium when he finally gave up, shrugging his shoulders as he sneaked out the side gate.

Back at school, he sought out Mr Carey and told him the news from Dr Shukla.

Carey grinned, and patted him on the back. 'That's fantastic, Madden, I'll see you for training at six.'

CHAPTER 25

The day before the game, another notice was pinned to the board outside the dining hall during breakfast. There, underneath the details for spectators who wanted to travel to the game, was an amended teamsheet. And there, beside 'No.12' was the name 'E. Madden'.

'Brilliant!' called out Alan. 'You're in the starting fifteen!'

Eoin smiled, and accepted the many pats that were rained on his back. He jumped back, however, when he saw a fist emerge between the cluster of friends, and crash into his ribs.

'Oi, that hurt,' he cried, turning towards the fist, which was on the end of the arm owned by Richie Duffy. The out-half bully was smirking.

'Hope the ribs are up to it, Madden,' he snapped. 'It's a big game for a little boy from Tipperagua.'

'The ribs are fine, Duffy, it was the other side that was cracked,' he chuckled.

The bully turned away, furious, and the rest of the boys joined in with Eoin's laughter.

Shortly before one o'clock the headmaster came over the PA to announce that there wouldn't be any classes in the afternoon and he hoped to see everyone at Lansdowne Road the next day. Mr McCaffrey also asked the cup final squad to come to his office after the final class.

Eoin joined the crowd as the boys marched up to the headmaster's study. It was a large room, with a long table used for meetings, upon which lay a mountain of tasty treats.

'All right, boys,' Mr McCaffrey announced, 'I know this isn't the healthiest approach to an important sporting event, but Mr Carey says you have done all the hard work and pizza and burgers won't do you much harm – *in moderation*. So do tuck in, but take it easy.'

The boys eyed up the foodstuffs they had been forbidden for months, and drooled. Eoin's pre-match nerves were starting to rumble, so he wasn't feeling very hungry, but hepicked up a slice of pizza to be polite.

'Thank you, sir,' he said as Mr McCaffrey came over to him.

'De-de-lisssshus,' gurgled Charlie Johnston through a mouthful of burger and bun.

'I hear you've been in the wars, Mr Madden,' the headmaster said, 'I presume you are fighting fit for the morrow?'

'Yes, sir, I had a rib injury, but it healed up quickly and I'll be fine.'

'That's quite a relief, I hear, to Mr Carey. He's terribly impressed with the progress you have made in such a short period of time. Is it true you never played rugby before you came to Castlerock? Less than six months and you're Mr Carey's main match-winner...'

'Well ...' Eoin mumbled, uncomfortable at the praise, which seemed to annoy Charlie, '... we have loads of great players and I've picked it up quickly from Mr Carey and Mr Finn.'

'Mr Finn?' said the headmaster, 'I thought he gave up coaching long ago?'

'No, well, yes, but ...' said Eoin, flustered, 'It's his book, I found it very helpful.'

'Oh, that old thing. Didn't know it was still in print. He forced us all to read it when it came out.'

To Eoin's great relief, the headmaster moved on to the next group of boys. Charlie looked at him with a serious expression.

'"The main match-winner"? Where did he get that from?'

'Well it wasn't from me!' Eoin said.

'Huh, you backs, always get the most attention when the real work is done in the forwards. I hope you guys appreciate all we do when you're collecting your medals tomorrow.'

After lunch Mr Carey got the boys to change into tracksuits and took them for a run around the school grounds.

'Let's get that pizza out of your systems before tomorrow. Brian O'Driscoll wouldn't eat such a thing before a big game.'

It was a subdued training session, with no real spark shown by any of the players. Mr Carey told them not to worry, that all the work had been done and they would be the best team on the field tomorrow. All they had to do was remember their plans and the scores would come.

Eoin wandered back to the school at the back of the group, and Mr Carey caught up with him.

'Everything all right, Madden?' he asked, looking straight into Eoin's eyes.

'I'm fine, sir, just a bit nervous. How many people will be there?'

'Get that out of your head, son, once the whistle blows you won't see or hear anyone except the black and blue shirts of St Osgur's. To be honest, I doubt if any of the Leinster supporters will come along until the last ten minutes, so you'll only have to worry about the mammies, daddies and little sisters shrieking in the crowd.'

'And grandads, of course,' said Mr Finn, who was standing on the steps of the school. 'I've just had the most wonderful phone call from Dixie, who told me the doctor has told him he is fit and well enough to travel. Your dad pulled some strings to get them nice seats in out of the cold, too.'

Eoin broke into a wide smile, delighted that his Grandad was obviously much better, and that he would get the chance to see him play at the national stadium.

'Wow,' he thought, before suddenly realising that his pre-match nerves had increased. 'I'll never sleep at all tonight.'

CHAPTER 26

Eoin need not have worried. It was still dark when he woke, but when he walked to the window to check his watch the sun was starting to make an appearance. He watched it for a few minutes, working out where it might be in the sky when the referee blew his whistle seven or eight hours hence.

'You all right, Eoin?' came a little voice behind him. 'Did you sleep much?'

'Like a baby,' Eoin replied, 'I'm just awake. Looks like a nice day for it.'

Alan jumped out of bed to check the skies. 'Big day for you, buddy. Are your folks coming up?'

'Yeah – and Grandad too.'

'Wow, we'll finally get to see the great Dixie Madden. Could you get me his autograph?'

Eoin stared at Alan. 'His autograph? Why?'

'You seem to take this grandad of yours for granted,'

Alan said, pointing at the plaque on the door. 'He's a genuine rugby legend.'

'Rugby legend? Did somebody call me?' chipped in Rory, who was standing by his bed yawning. 'Today's the day the world discovers the great Rory Grehan!'

Eoin looked at Alan and frowned. Rory was losing the run of himself. He was lucky to have made the team, but he now thought he was God's gift to rugby. The Aviva Stadium was no place to discover your limitations.

The team ate breakfast together, and went for a fifteen-minute jog afterwards. It was a sunny morning, but cold, and as they arrived back at the school Eoin noticed an old man sitting in a wheelchair submerged in a sea of blankets.

'Grandad,' he cried, rushing over to where his family had parked their car. The rest of the team stopped, and all stared at one of Castlerock's rugby legends.

'It is a great pleasure to meet you, sir,' said Mr Carey, shaking Dixie's hand, 'and particularly on a day of such honour for the Madden family. To see your grandson play at Lansdowne Road must be a great thrill for you.'

'Oh it is indeed,' said Dixie, 'I'm very proud of young Eoin, you have done a fine job on his rugby.'

Mr Carey smiled, not a regular habit of his at all. 'Well, Mr Madden, there's something about the lad that shows me that there's got to be something in his genes too.'

Mr Finn walked down the steps to greet his old friend, and Eoin made his farewells, explaining that he had a team meeting and a walk on Sandymount Strand before they arrived at the stadium.

Dixie called him aside before he left, 'Remember, Eoin,' he whispered. 'This is only a sport. A fantastic one, but one you can leave behind when you walk off the field. You will do your very best, I know, because that's the sort of lad you are. And whatever happens, you've made your mum, dad and me very proud.'

Eoin turned away quickly, not wanting to show that he was blinking back tears.

The morning flew past, with Mr Carey talking them through their previous games and the moves that had brought them tries. He pointed out the silly mistakes that had cost them points, too, but told the team they had learned from those errors and would not be making them today. He kept hammering home to Richie Duffy that he had a talented backline behind him and he needed to get the ball to them as much as possible.

Mr McCaffrey took the team on a leisurely stroll across the beach, telling them that this was a Castlerock tradition that went back more than a century.

'Mr Finn was telling us about the days he walked

here with Dixie Madden, and how they strolled up to Lansdowne Road from here. You boys have a nice bus to take you, of course, but don't forget that Dixie and Mr Finn will be there today cheering you on. Tradition is an important thing in rugby, and in Castlerock. Today you all become part of that tradition.'

Eoin had a lump in his throat as the bus drove across Herbert Bridge and on to Lansdowne Road. The bus pulled into the tunnel where he had last met Brian, and he briefly wondered where his friend had gone.

Castlerock settled into their dressing-room, but it was clear almost all the boys were overawed by the occasion.

'Just think,' said Charlie, 'Jonny Sexton took his socks off just where I'm sitting.'

'Bet his don't stink as much as yours,' roared Lorcan across the room.

'Settle down, lads,' said Mr Carey, who was just as impressed with the facilities. 'I should have brought the DVD of the semi-final to show you,' he said, pointing at the state-of-the-art TV system built into the wall.

'Can we watch *Spongebob Squarepants* instead?' asked Rory, with a grin.

The whole squad changed into their green and white Castlerock kit, did their warm-ups in the adjacent room, and all stood when the headmaster came in with Mr

Finn, who he asked to say a few words.

'Well, boys, today is the biggest day of your rugby lives so far,' he started. 'It is a great honour for you to represent the school in this final, and in this marvellous stadium. I know you won't let yourselves or the school down, but do make sure you enjoy yourselves. Some of you may never get the chance to play here again, so make the most of this day. All your family, friends and schoolmates are behind you. And so are scores of Castlerock players of the past. From the very heart of one of them, I wish you the very best of luck. And remember, *Victoria Concordia Crescit* – Victory comes from harmony.'

CHAPTER 27

The Castlerock boys waited in the tunnel alongside their opponents from St Osgur's. As the teams looked around, sizing up their surroundings and each other, a harsh electronic voice came crackling in through the open end of the archway. The stadium announcer was making his first message of the day welcoming the fans, before he said, 'And here they come, the teams that are about to do battle for the Fr Geoghegan Cup.'

'Off you go,' grinned the attendant, 'There's a full house outside waiting for you.'

Rory looked at Eoin and gulped, but when they burst out into the sunshine they were relieved to see that the official was only joking. There was a thin smattering of fans in the vast arena.

'Maybe two thousand,' said Rory, gazing all around. 'But that's still an awful lot for an Under 13 schools match.'

'It'll be an awful lot more by the end,' said the outside centre Phelim Hardiman, jogging from one end of the field to the other and soaking up the atmosphere.

Eoin looked across to where the Castlerock supporters had gathered, and gave a wave. He then remembered his grandad wouldn't be with the schoolboys, and scanned the hospitality boxes before he found his family. They saluted him, and he lifted his hand in acknowledgement.

The pre-match warm-ups complete, the teams settled into formation and awaited the referee's whistle.

St Osgur's College was a big school in the city centre and had a long rivalry with Castlerock. Its players were fast, well-drilled by a former Ireland winger who had a spell coaching one of Dublin's best clubs. In the early minutes they got the ball out to their backs as often as they could, but Castlerock's defence held firm.

A garryowen was driven high in the air by the St Osgur's full-back, and Eoin found himself beneath the ball. Ever since that first training session when he became a laughing stock, Eoin had been solid under the high ball. It was something he prided himself on. But now, in the biggest game of his short life, Eoin fluffed it.

The ball bounced off his chest and, although he

scrambled forward to try to catch it, it tumbled to the ground.

The referee whistled, calling out 'knock on'.

'Catch the ball, Madden,' hissed Duffy, glaring at Eoin.

From the scrum, St Osgur's worked the ball out at speed to their winger, who skipped past Lorcan and went over in the corner.

The team gathered under the posts for the conversion.

'For God's sake, let's cut out the stupid mistakes,' snarled Duffy. Eoin went red, knowing it was he who had made the error. He looked over at the giant scoreboard, where a number '7' twice as tall as Mr Carey had just appeared beside 'St Osgur's'.

'Lay off, Duffy,' said Charlie. 'Eoin's a class player, that's the first ball he's dropped all season.'

Three or four of the players muttered agreement.

Duffy was taken aback at this show of defiance from a team he had always had under his thumb.

'OK, let's get on with it,' he said, 'and remember the moves.'

Coming up to half-time, St Osgur's kicked a penalty to stretch their lead to 10-0, before the most important moment of the game arrived.

The Castlerock forwards had won the ball in the ruck, and were keeping it tight as the backs found their best attacking formation. Rory bent to pick up the ball, and dummied to fling it out to Duffy. The big St Osgur's second row broke off the ruck and charged straight at the Castlerock out-half.

The sounds of their collision echoed around the vast arena, which was still almost empty.

Thump!

Crrrrack!

'Aaaaaaaahhhhh!'

Both teams stopped dead, staring at the stricken player lying on the ground clutching his arm.

'Aaaaaaaahhhhh!' he howled again, as the coach and doctor rushed on.

Duffy had turned white, and looked terrified.

'I think it's, broken, sir,' he said. 'I heard it crack.'

The St John's Ambulance boys followed out on to the pitch and helped the doctor to lift Duffy carefully on to the stretcher.

With just a few seconds left to the interval, the referee allowed just enough time for play to resume before blowing for half-time.

Both sides were subdued as they wandered up the tunnel, but Castlerock's fourteen men were completely silent.

'All right boys, Richie is in good hands now,' said Mr

Carey. 'He'll be fine and so will we. We've been a bit unlucky so far, but once you guys hit your stride the scores will come.'

'O'Reilly, you warm-up,' he said, 'I'll slot you in at inside centre. Madden, you move into out-half. You'll be taking the place kicks, too.'

All eyes turned to Eoin. Everyone knew about his year-long feud with Duffy, and most people now sympathised with Eoin. But to be taking the prized No.10 position in these circumstances just didn't seem right.

Eoin nodded, afraid to say anything.

He stood up, and checked the clock, there were six minutes left before the second half.

'I need to use the bathroom, sir,' he said.

He headed straight for the cubicle situated furthest from the changing area and sat down and put his head in his hands.

'What's up, soldier?' came a voice from outside the door.

'Brian!' said Eoin, 'Where have you been? I called over last week.'

'Long story, pal, but I'm not going to be around here much longer. It seems the fact that you were the first person to be able to see me woke up, eh, *some people* up

to my presence here. They can't have that hap[pening]
so I'm off to a better place – if you can imagine su[ch a]
thing,' he grinned.

'So, I won't see you again?' said Eoin.

'No, I'm afraid not,' replied Brian.

Eoin left the cubicle and looked at the ghostly figure, who already seemed as if he was starting to fade.

'I've enjoyed our chats, and you really helped me reconnect with rugby – and Tipperary – again. But it's not right that I'm hanging around here for eighty years so I'll be off soon. They told me I could stay to watch your game, and I'll be with you all the way,' said Brian.

Eoin bit his lip. 'Did you see that injury to Duffy? The coach has asked me to fill in at out-half. I'm terrified.'

'Don't be,' said Brian. 'You're a fantastic player with great natural skills. The ball will be coming to you a bit quicker, but trust your instincts and you'll be fine. That team you're playing has their defence all bunched in the middle of the field: get the ball out to your wingers and you'll get the tries.'

'Thanks,' said Eoin, greatly cheered. 'There's a man in the hospitality box near the twenty-two that you should take a look at. It's the great Dixie Madden.'

'That's a name from the past,' smiled Brian, 'Just like mine. But yours is one for the future – so go out there and win that cup for your school.'

CHAPTER 28

Eoin rushed back to the changing room, where he apologised to Mr Carey for the delay. 'Nerves, sir,' he muttered.

'OK, lads, settle down. We'll keep it simple and concentrate on cutting out the errors. You are Castlerock boys; you have everything you need to win this game. So go out and do it.'

Eoin walked out to the middle of the ground alone. The referee tossed him the ball, which he placed on the white line and kicked off towards the Havelock Square End.

A perfect drop kick was followed up by the forwards and the ball was taken cleanly. The pack were growing in confidence and having worked the ball up to the 22-metre line, Charlie picked up the ball and charged straight at the posts. Taken aback by his sheer neck, St Osgur's hesitated and he was only three yards from the line when they finally brought him to ground.

'Brilliant, Chaz, just brilliant,' chuckled Eoin as the Castlerock pack piled in to support their comrade.

Charlie had turned his body as he fell so the ball was on the attacking side, and Brendan picked it up and fed it back through his legs. Rory stood over the ball, deciding which way to pass, when Eoin nodded and pointed where he wanted the ball.

Rory flung the ball far in front of his out-half, but Eoin moved like lightning to run onto it, sidestep the St Osgur's cover and dive over the line for a try.

He took the congratulations of his teammates before he turned to compose himself for the conversion. He struck the ball well, but a late gust of wind pushed it out to the right. Eoin held his breath as the ball hit the inside of the post and dropped down. The touch judges looked at each other and raised their flags – Castlerock were back within touching distance at 10-7.

But any thoughts that St Osgur's would cave in were short-lived. They held steady as Castlerock tried to break through their solid defence, and began to come back into the game.

An Osgur's attack down the right was held up on the 22, but Brendan came into the ruck from the side and the referee blew for a penalty.

'We'll kick it,' said the St Osgur's out-half, who duly slotted the ball over to extend their lead to six points.

Castlerock came roaring back, but chance after chance was wasted and with two minutes left they were still without reward. They were awarded a scrum on half-way, but there was a delay as a St Osgur's player received treatment on an injured ankle.

Eoin supped from a bottle of water, and stared up high into the stands where the Leinster supporters were starting to take their seats ahead of the second big game of the day.

Just to the left of the box where his family were seated he spied Brian, his distinctive black, red and gold jersey standing out in a sea of blue. Brian stretched his arms wide, pointing to the wings. Eoin remembered his tip at half-time. It was worth trying.

'Listen, guys,' he told the backs, 'their backs are all bunched up in the middle, let's get the ball out to Joseph and Shane on the wings.'

Castlerock got a good heel from the scrum, and Charlie again controlled the ball between his feet. Rory plunged down, and threw the ball out quickly to Eoin, who ran ten metres before flinging the ball out far to his right. He had deliberately skipped Mikey O'Reilly at inside centre and the surprise move fooled St Osgur's.

Phelim moved the ball on quickly to Shane Keane, and the winger suddenly discovered he was on his own in a vast area of free space. Shane was the fastest runner in the whole year at school, and he wasn't going to be caught by anyone, especially with a ten-metre start.

He sprinted towards the posts and, with a cheeky dive, touched the ball down beneath them to bring the score to 13-12.

The crowd – which by this stage had swelled to more than twenty-five thousand – erupted. 'Cas-tle-rock, Cas-tle-rock,' they shouted, even the neutrals.

'What's left, ref?' asked Eoin.

'Nothing, son,' he smiled. 'This is the last kick of the game. Good luck.'

Eoin collected the ball from Shane, who was grinning from ear to ear. 'Best of luck, Eoin, you'd kick this in your sleep.'

'Thanks,' muttered Eoin under his breath, 'no pressure then.'

Shane was right, of course, but he didn't realise how nervous Eoin had suddenly become. The out-half was totally aware of what was at stake – and that enormous roar that greeted the try was the first time he had real-ised how many people were now watching.

He knelt on one knee to prop the ball up on the

kicking tee. He looked towards the posts, and was startled to see Brian standing underneath them, just beside the touch judges.

'Come on now, Eoin,' he called out, 'take your time, keep your eyes wide open and keep everything steady.'

Eoin smiled, and stared up at the white posts piercing the blue sky high above the stadium. He stepped back to his mark, and ran forwards, keeping his eye on where he was going to kick the ball.

Whump!

Eoin connected perfectly with the ball, and watched as it took off into the air, he knew it was straight and he knew it was true. The touch judges lifted their little flags and the referee blew his whistle, followed immediately by yet another blast.

That was the last thing Eoin heard before he was swamped by a sea of green and white shirts.

'Oi, mind me ribs,' he cried out, as the delighted teammates hugged him and each other in victory.

The boys ran around like lunatics for five minutes, before a delighted Mr Carey called them together. 'OK lads, that was fantastic. I'm so proud of you all. Now go over and shake hands with every one of the St Osgur's lads and let's collect this cup. Jonny Sexton wants to get out here to play and we're holding him up!'

Richie Duffy came onto the field, his arm strapped up in a sling. 'Well done lads,' he said, '... even The Bogger.' Eoin looked at him, and suddenly felt a bit sorry for him.

'Yeah, thanks, Duffy, we missed you today.'

The players looked around at each other, no one daring to be the one to laugh first.

'Ha, ha, ha,' roared Rory, 'good one, Eoin.'

'Yeah, good one,' grinned Duffy. 'Thanks for keeping my position warm, Madden, and well done today. But I'll be back in No.10 next season.'

Eoin smiled, and pointed at the enormous silver cup sitting on a table in front of the West Stand, 'Well then, I hope you can carry that with one arm. Give me a shout if you need a hand.'

The team collected their medals, and Eoin clutched his tight in his hand as he waved towards his family. Dixie lifted his hand and waved back. Eoin could see his grin from fifty yards away.

The Leinster branch president presented the cup to Duffy, who did struggle to hold it up without help. The team took turns to lift it over their heads, and jogged over to the Castlerock fans where they received an enormous cheer.

'Right, lads,' said Mr Carey when they got back to the

dressing room. 'You can stay to watch the Leinster game if you like, and then we'll all meet back at the school at 7.30pm for a party. Nothing too fancy now, but bring your families along too.'

Eoin left his playing shirt on, but got changed quickly and took the steps three at a time up to the hospitality level. He didn't have a ticket, but the steward recognised him from his starring performance out on the pitch.

'Eoin, you were fantastic,' said Dixie, looking happier than Eoin ever remembered seeing him.

'Thanks, Grandad, I actually enjoyed playing out-half after a while.'

'And what possessed you to make that long pass at the end? That was truly brilliant.'

'Well ...' Eoin hesitated, 'I suppose you're right. I must have been possessed.'

'Do you know, Dixie,' said Andy Finn, 'I don't think I've seen a better display for the school in the No.10 shirt since the last time it was worn by a boy called Madden.'

Eoin bent to hug his Grandad, and saw he was clutching a large book.

'It's an album of photographs of every team I ever played on,' Dixie said. 'Andy here had them all, of course, and he arranged to have copies made. Look at that –

two handsome fellows weren't we?'

Eoin grinned.

He turned to look out on the arena below, and watched as the Leinster stars ran out onto the field. This was a great game, and a magical place. He looked over at the posts where he had kicked the winning points, and where he had last seen Brian, and he smiled.

AUTHOR'S NOTE

The character of Brian in *Rugby Spirit* is based on a real rugby player, Brian Hanrahan, who died in 1927. All the references to his life and death are based on real events. His story is told in the chapter 'The Fatal Scrum' in *Lansdowne Road: the Stadium, the Matches, the Greatest Days* by Gerard Siggins & Malachy Clerkin (O'Brien Press 2010). All other references to people, alive or dead, are fictional.

TURN THE PAGE TO

SAMPLE

RUGBY WARRIOR

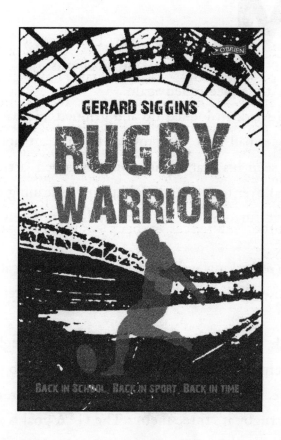

CHAPTER 1

'Mind the cow pats, Eoin!' came the call from behind the goalposts. 'Ah … too late …' the voice called again.

Eoin Madden looked up and grinned. He had been kicking a ball over the crossbar for half an hour, but hadn't seen his grandfather, Dixie Madden, arrive. He rambled over to where the old man was leaning on the rail that surrounded the Ormondstown Gaels GAA pitch.

'You're kicking well,' said Dixie, 'but it's cheating to use those Gaelic posts – they're a good bit lower, aren't they?'

'Yeah, I suppose so,' said Eoin, picking the rugby ball up carefully from where it sat atop a crusty slab of cow manure. 'The crossbar is two and a half metres high, and in rugby it's three metres. The GAA goal is a good bit wider too, but sure it's good practice and it's quiet here today.'

'Your mother tells me you're getting ready to get back up to Castlerock next week?'

'I suppose I am,' replied Eoin. 'I had a great summer and the Gaels had a good run in the championship too, but I really missed the rugby, to be honest. I must be the only thirteen-year-old in the country who can't wait for the holidays to end and to get back to school!'

'Well, you look like you're getting back in the groove,' grinned Dixie. 'That last kick was as good as the one you made to win the Father Geoghegan Cup.'

'That was a great day, wasn't it?' Eoin replied, with a smile. 'I'd love to play in the Aviva again someday.'

'I must say, that whole day was a huge tonic,' said Dixie. 'I was treated like royalty and then to cap it all you really showed some class to keep your nerve for the kick. I was just looking at the scrapbook last night, because Andy Finn sent me on some great photos of the game I'll have to put into it. Maybe you'll give me a hand with that tonight?' he asked.

'I'd like that,' said Eoin, 'but I've set myself a target of a hundred kicks this afternoon and I have a few more to go, so I'd better get back to work now if that's OK?'

Dixie laughed and waved him back to his mark. 'That's some dedication, Eoin; mind you don't wear down the toe of that boot before the season starts!' before he wandered away towards his car.

Eoin teed up the ball a bit further away on the right, and gave himself a more difficult angle, but still split the posts. 'Huh, smaller target my eye,' he muttered to himself, 'I'd put them over even if it was half the width!'

He carried on with his practice for another ten minutes before he was interrupted again. This time it was a new Ormondstown Gaels team-mate called Dylan.

'Howya, Eoin,' chirped Dylan, who was about a foot smaller than Eoin and wore his hair shorter than a tennis ball.

'I'm grand, Dylan, what's going on with you?'

'I've a bit of news actually. I'm off to Dublin next week – they're sending me to Castlerock. Isn't that where you go?'

'It is indeed, that's great news. It'll be good to have another bogger to share the loudmouth Leinster fans with!'

Dylan looked a bit nervous. 'I'm not sure about that, I'm Leinster myself – Drogheda – don't they teach you Geography up in Castlerock? Leinster's not just about Blackrock and Dublin 4 you know. So, if you're getting grief for being a Munster fan then you're still on your own,' he grinned.

'Ha, thanks a bunch, pal! Are you any use at the rugby? It's pretty big up there in Castlerock.'

'Yeah, we lived in Limerick for a while too, so I picked it up. I wasn't bad at scrum-half they told me.'

'Well I didn't have you marked out as a second row, anyway, unless they've started a Smurfs rugby team …' laughed Eoin, as he skipped out of the way of Dylan's lame attempt to throw a punch. 'I'll see you before you go, and give you the lowdown on what to expect. But I've got to dash, just remembered Mam told me to be home early. It's fish pie tonight.'

And with that Eoin picked up his ball and shot out of the Gaelic grounds as fast as his legs could carry him.